William Livingston Alden

The adventures of Jimmy Brown

William Livingston Alden

The adventures of Jimmy Brown

ISBN/EAN: 9783743322363

Manufactured in Europe, USA, Canada, Australia, Japa

Cover: Foto ©Andreas Hilbeck / pixelio.de

Manufactured and distributed by brebook publishing software
(www.brebook.com)

William Livingston Alden

The adventures of Jimmy Brown

UNEXPECTED RESULTS OF JIMMY'S EFFORTS TO TRAP PIGS.   [*Page* 182.

The
Adventures of Jimmy Brown

WRITTEN BY HIMSELF

AND EDITED

BY W. L. ALDEN

ILLUSTRATED

NEW YORK AND LONDON
HARPER & BROTHERS PUBLISHERS
1902

CONTENTS.

Contents.

ILLUSTRATIONS.

Illustrations.

THE

ADVENTURES OF JIMMY BROWN.

MR. MARTIN'S GAME.

WHAT if he is a great deal older than I am! that doesn't give him any right to rumple my hair, does it? I'm willing to respect old age, of course, but I want my hair respected too.

But rumpling hair isn't enough for Mr. Martin; he must call me "Bub," and "Sonny." I might stand "Sonny," but I won't stand being called "Bub" by any living man —not if I can help it. I've told him three or four times "My name isn't 'Bub,' Mr. Martin. My name's Jim, or Jimmy," but he would just grin in an exhausperating kind of way, and keep on calling me "Bub."

My sister Sue doesn't like him any better than I do. He comes to see her about twice a week, and I've heard her say, "Goodness me there's that tiresome old bachelor again." But she treats him just as polite as she does anybody; and when he brings her candy, she says, "Oh Mr. Martin you are *too* good." There's a great deal of make-believe about girls, I think.

Now that I've mentioned candy, I will say that he might pass it around, but he never thinks of such a thing. Mr. Travers, who is the best of all Sue's young men, always brings candy with him, and gives me a lot. Then he generally gives me a quarter to go to the post-office for him, because he forgot to go, and expects something very important. It takes an hour to go to the post-office and back, but I'd do anything for such a nice man.

One night—it was Mr. Travers's regular night—Mr. Martin came, and wasn't Sue mad! She knew Mr. Travers would come in about half an hour, and she always made it a rule to keep her young men separate.

She sent down word that she was busy, and would be down-stairs after a while. Would Mr. Martin please sit down and wait. So he sat down on the front piazza and waited.

I was sitting on the grass, practising mumble-te-peg a little, and by-and-by Mr. Martin says, "Well, Bub, what are you doing?"

"Playing a game," says I. "Want to learn it?"

"Well, I don't care if I do," says he. So he came out and sat on the grass, and I showed him how to play.

Just then Mr. Travers arrived, and Sue came down, and was awfully glad to see both her friends. "But what in the world are you doing?" she says to Mr. Martin. When she heard that he was learning the game, she said, "How interesting do play one game."

Mr. Martin finally said he would. So we played a game, and I let him beat me very easy. He laughed fit to kill himself when I drew the peg, and said it was the best game he ever played.

"Is there any game you play any better than this, Sonny?" said he, in his most irragravating style.

"Let's have another game," said I. "Only you must promise to draw the peg fair, if I beat you."

"All right," said he. "I'll draw the peg if you beat me, Bub."

O, he felt so sure he was a first-class player. I don't like a conceited man, no matter if he is only a boy.

You can just imagine how quick I beat him. Why, I went right through to "both ears" without stopping, and the first time I threw the knife over my head it stuck in the ground.

I cut a beautiful peg out of hard wood—one of those sharp, slender pegs that will go through anything but a stone. I drove it in clear out of sight, and Mr. Martin, says he, "Why, Sonny, nobody couldn't possibly draw that peg."

"I've drawn worse pegs than that," said I. "You've got to clear away the earth with your chin and front teeth, and then you can draw it."

"That is nonsense," said Mr. Martin, growing red in the face.

"This is a fair and square game," says I, "and you gave your word to draw the peg if I beat you."

"I do hope Mr. Martin will play fair," said Sue. "It would be too bad to cheat a little boy."

So Mr. Martin got down and tried it, but he didn't like it one bit. "See here, Jimmy," said he, "I'll give you half a dollar, and we'll consider the peg drawn."

"That is bribery and corruption," said I. "Mr. Martin, I can't be bribed, and didn't think you'd try to hire me to let you break your promise."

When he saw I wouldn't let up on him, he got down again and went to work.

It was the best fun I ever knew. I just rolled on the ground and laughed till I cried. Sue and Mr. Travers didn't roll, but they laughed till Sue got up and ran into the house, where I could hear her screaming on the front-parlor sofa, and mother crying out, "My darling child where does it hurt you won't you have the doctor Jane do bring the camphor."

Mr. Martin gnawed away at the earth, and used swear-words to himself, and was perfectly raging. After a while he got the peg, and then he got up with his face about the color of a flower-pot, and put on his hat and went out of the front gate rubbing his face with his handkerchief, and never so much as saying good-night. He didn't come near the house again for two weeks.

Mr. Travers gave me a half-dollar to go to the post-office to make up for the one I had refused, and told me that I had displayed roaming virtue, though I don't know exactly what he meant.

He looked over this story, and corrected the spelling for me, only it is to be a secret that he helped me. I'd do almost anything for him, and I'm going to ask Sue to marry him just to please me.

MR. MARTIN'S SCALP.

After that game of mumble-te-peg that me and Mr. Martin played, he did not come to our house for two weeks. Mr. Travers said perhaps the earth he had to gnaw while he was drawing the peg had struck to his insides and made him sick, but I knew it couldn't be that. I've drawn pegs that were drove into every kind of earth, and it never hurt me. Earth is healthy, unless it is lime; and don't you ever let anybody drive a peg into lime. If you were to swallow the least bit of lime, and then drink some water, it would burn a hole through you just as quick as anything. There was once a boy who found some lime in the closet, and thought it was sugar, and of course he didn't like the taste of it. So he drank some water to take the taste out of his mouth, and pretty soon his mother said, " I smell something burning goodness gracious the house is on fire." But the boy he gave a dreadful scream, and said, " Ma, it's me !" and the smoke curled up out of his pockets and around his neck, and he burned up and died. I know this is true, because Tom McGinnis went to school with him, and told me about it.

Mr. Martin came to see Susan last night for the first time since we had our game; and I wish he had never come back, for he got me into an awful scrape. This was the way it happened. I was playing Indian in the yard. I had a wooden tomahawk and a wooden scalping-knife and a bow-narrow. I was dressed up in father's old coat turned inside out, and had six chicken feathers in my hair. I was playing I was Green Thunder, the Delaware chief, and was hunting for pale-faces in the yard. It was just after supper, and I was having a real nice time, when Mr. Travers came, and he said, "Jimmy, what are you up to now?" So I told him I was Green Thunder, and was on the war-path. Said he, "Jimmy, I think I saw Mr. Martin on his way here. Do you think you would mind scalping him?" I said I wouldn't scalp him for nothing, for that would be cruelty; but if Mr. Travers was sure that Mr. Martin was the enemy of the red man, then Green Thunder's heart would ache for revenge, and I would scalp him with pleasure. Mr. Travers said that Mr. Martin was a notorious enemy and oppressor of the Indians, and he gave me ten cents, and said that as soon as Mr. Martin should come and be sitting comfortably on the piazza, I was to give the war-whoop and scalp him.

Well, in a few minutes Mr. Martin came, and he and Mr. Travers and Susan sat on the piazza, and talked as if they were all so pleased to see each other, which was the highest-pocracy in the world. After a while Mr. Martin saw me, and said, "How silly boys are! that boy makes believe he's an Indian, and he knows he's only a little nuisance." Now this made me mad, and I thought I would give him a good scare, just to teach him not to call names if a fellow does beat him in a fair game. So I began to steal softly up the piazza steps, and to get around behind him. When I had got about six feet from him I gave a warwhoop, and jumped at him. I caught hold of his scalp-lock with one hand, and drew my wooden scalping-knife around his head with the other.

I never got such a fright in my whole life. The knife was that dull that it wouldn't have cut butter; but, true as I sit here, Mr. Martin's whole scalp came right off in my hand. I thought I had killed him, and I dropped his scalp, and said, "For mercy's sake! I didn't go to do it, and I'm awfully sorry." But he just caught up his scalp, stuffed it in his pocket, and jammed his hat on his head, and walked off, saying to Susan, "I didn't come here to be insulted by a little wretch that deserves the gallows."

Mr. Travers and Susan never said a word until he had gone, and then they laughed until the noise brought father out to ask what was the matter. When he heard what had happened, instead of laughing, he looked very angry, said that "Mr. Martin was a worthy man. My son, you may come up-stairs with me."

If you've ever been a boy, you know what happened up-stairs, and I needn't say any more on a very painful subject. I didn't mind it so much, for I thought Mr. Martin would die, and then I would be hung, and put in jail; but before she went to bed Susan came and whispered through the door that it was all right; that Mr. Martin was made that way, so he could be taken apart easy, and that I hadn't hurt him. I shall have to stay in my room all day to-day, and eat bread and water; and what I say is that if men are made with scalps that may come off any minute if a boy just touches them, it isn't fair to blame the boy.

A PRIVATE CIRCUS.

THERE's going to be a circus here, and I'm going to it; that is, if father will let me. Some people think it's wrong to go to a circus, but I don't. Mr. Travers says that the mind of man and boy requires circuses in moderation, and that the wicked boys in Sunday-school books who steal their employers' money to buy circus tickets wouldn't steal it if their employers, or their fathers or uncles, would give them circus tickets once in a while. I'm sure I wouldn't want to go to a circus every night in the week. All I should want would be to go two or three evenings, and Wednesday and Saturday afternoons. There was once a boy who was awfully fond of going to the circus, and his employer, who was a very good man, said he'd cure him. So he said to the boy, "Thomas, my son, I'm going to hire you to go to the circus every night. I'll pay you three dollars a week, and give you your board and lodging, if you'll go every night except Sunday; but if you don't go, then you won't get any board and lodging or any money." And the boy said, "Oh, you can just bet I'll go!" and he thought everything was lovely; but after two weeks he got so sick of the circus that he would have given anything to be let to stay away. Finally he got so wretched that he deceived his good employer, and stole money from him to buy school-books with, and ran away and went to school. The older he grew the more he looked back with horror upon that awful period when he went to the circus every night. Mr. Travers says it finally had such an effect upon him that he worked hard all day and read books all night just to keep it out of his mind. The result was that before he knew it he became a very learned and a very rich man. Of course it was very wrong for the boy to steal money to stay away from the circus with, but the story teaches us that if we go to the circus too much, we shall get tired of it, which is a very solemn thing.

We had a private circus at our house last night—at least that's what father called it, and he seemed to enjoy it. It happened in this way. I went into the back parlor one evening, because I wanted to see Mr. Travers. He and Sue always sit there. It was growing quite dark when I went in, and going towards the sofa, I happened to walk against a rocking-chair that was rocking all by itself, which, come to think of it, was an awfully curious thing, and I'm going to ask somebody about it. I didn't mind walking into the chair, for it didn't hurt me much, only I knocked it over, and it hit Sue, and she said, "Oh my get me something quick!" and then fainted away. Mr. Travers was dreadfully frightened, and said, "Run, Jimmy, and get the cologne, or the bay-rum, or something." So I ran up to Sue's room, and felt round in the dark for her bottle of cologne that she always keeps on her bureau. I found a bottle after a minute or two, and ran down and gave it to Mr. Travers, and he bathed Sue's face as well as he could in the dark, and she came to and said, "Goodness gracious do you want to put my eyes out?"

Just then the front-door bell rang, and Mr. Bradford (our new minister) and his wife and three daughters and his son came in. Sue jumped up and ran into the front parlor to light the gas, and Mr. Travers came to help her. They just got it lit when the visitors came in, and father and mother came down-stairs to meet them. Mr. Bradford looked as if he had seen a ghost, and his wife and daughters said, "Oh my!" and father said, "What on earth!" and mother just burst out laughing, and said, "Susan, you and Mr. Travers seem to have had an accident with the ink-stand."

You never saw such a sight as those poor young people were. I had made a mistake, and brought down a bottle of liquid blacking. Mr. Travers had put it all over Sue's face, so that she was jet black, all but a little of one cheek

"OH, MY !"

and the end of her nose; and then he had rubbed his hands on his own face until he was like an Ethiopian leopard, only he could change his spots if he used soap enough.

You couldn't have any idea how angry Sue was with me —just as if it was my fault, when all I did was to go up-stairs for her, and get a bottle to bring her to with; and it would have been all right if she hadn't left the blacking-bottle on her bureau; and I don't call that tidy, if she is a girl. Mr. Travers wasn't a bit angry; but he came up to my room and washed his face, and laughed all the time. And Sue got awfully angry with him, and said she would never speak to him again after disgracing her in that heartless way. So he went home, and I could hear him laughing all the way down the street, and Mr. Bradford and his folks thought that he and Sue had been having a minstrel show, and mother thinks they'll never come to the house again.

As for father, he was almost as much amused as Mr. Travers, and he said it served Sue right, and he wasn't go-ing to punish the boy to please her. I'm going to try to have another circus some day, though this one was all an accident, and of course I was dreadfully sorry about it.

BURGLARS.

Some people are afraid of burglars. Girls are awfully afraid of them. When they think there's a burglar in the house, they pull the clothes over their heads and scream "Murder father Jimmy there's a man in the house call the police fire!" just as if that would do any good. What you ought to do if there is a burglar is to get up and shoot him with a double-barrelled gun and then tie him and send the servant out to tell the police that if they will call after breakfast you will have something ready for them that will please them. I shouldn't be a bit frightened if I woke up and found a strange man in my room. I should just pretend that I was asleep and keep watching him and when he went to climb out of the window and got half way out I'd jump up and shut the window down on him and tie his legs. But you can't expect girls to have any courage, or to know what to do when anything happens.

We had been talking about burglars one day last week just before I went to bed, and I thought I would put my bownarrow where it would be handy if a robber did come

It is a nice strong bow, and I had about thirty arrows with sharp points in the end about half an inch long, that I made out of some big black pins that Susan had in her pin-cushion. My room is in the third story, just over Sue's room, and the window comes right down on the floor, so that you can lie on the floor and put your head out. I couldn't go to sleep that night very well, though I ate about a quart of chestnuts after I went to bed and I've heard mother say that if you eat a little something delicate late at night it will make you go to sleep.

· A long while after everybody had gone to bed I heard two men talking in a low tone under the window, and I jumped up to see what was the matter. Two dreadful ruffians were standing under Sue's window, and talking so low that it was a wonder I could hear anything.

One of them had something that looked like a tremendous big squash, with a long neck, and the other had something that looked like a short crowbar. It didn't take me long to understand what they were going to do. The man with the crowbar was intending to dig a hole in the foundation of the house and then the other man would put the big squash which was full of dynamighty in the hole and light a slow-match and run away and blow the house to pieces. So I thought the best thing would be to shoot them before they could do their dreadful work.

I got my bownarrow and laid down on the floor and took a good aim at one of the burglars. I hit him in the leg, and he said, "Ow! ow! I've run a thorn mornamile into my leg."

Then I gave the other fellow an arrow, and he said, "My goodness this place is full of thorns, there's one in my leg too."

Then they moved back a little and I began to shoot as fast as ever I could. I hit them every time, and they were frightened to death. The fellow with the thing like a squash dropped it on the ground and the other fellow jumped on it just as I hit him in the cheek and smashed it all to pieces. You can just believe that they did not stay in our yard very long. They started for the front gate on a run, yelling "Ow! ow!" and I am sorry to say using the worst kind of swear-words. The noise woke up father and he lit the gas and I saw the two wretches in the street picking the arrows out of each other but they ran off as soon as they saw the light.

Father says that they were not burglars at all, but were only two idiots that had come to serenade Sue; but when I asked him what serenading was he said it was far worse than burglary, so I know the men were the worst kind of robbers. I found a broken guitar in the yard the next morning, and there wasn't anything in it that would explode, but it would have been very easy for the robbers to have filled it with something that would have blown the house to atoms. I suppose they preferred to put it in a guitar so that if they met anybody nobody would suspect anything.

Neither mother nor Sue showed any gratitude to me for saving their lives, though father did say that for once that boy had showed a little sense.

When Mr. Travers came that evening and I told him about it he said, "Jimmy! there's such a thing as being just a little too smart."

I don't know what he meant, but I suppose he was a little cross, for he had hurt himself some way—he wouldn't tell me how—and had court-plaster on his cheek and on his hands and walked as if his legs were stiff. Still, if a man doesn't feel well he needn't be rude.

MR. MARTIN'S EYE.

I've made up my mind to one thing, and that is, I'll never have anything to do with Mr. Martin again. He ought to be ashamed of himself, going around and getting boys into scrapes, just because he's put together so miserably. Sue says she believes it's mucilage, and I think she's right. If he couldn't afford to get himself made like other people, why don't he stay at home? His father and mother must have been awfully ashamed of him. Why, he's liable to fall apart at any time, Mr. Travers says, and some of these days he'll have to be swept up off the floor and carried home in three or four baskets.

There was a ghost one time who used to go around, up-stairs and down-stairs, in an old castle, carrying his head in his hand, and stopping in front of everybody he met, but never saying a word. This frightened all the people dreadfully, and they couldn't get a servant to stay in the house unless she had the policeman to sit up in the kitchen with her all night. One day a young doctor came to stay at the castle, and said he didn't believe in ghosts, and that nobody ever saw a ghost, unless they had been making beasts of themselves with mince-pie and wedding-cake. So the old lord of the castle he smiled very savage, and said, " You'll believe in ghosts before you've been in this castle twenty-four hours, and don't you forget it." Well, that very night the ghost came into the young doctor's room and woke him up. The doctor looked at him, and said, " Ah, I perceive: painful case of imputation of the neck. Want it cured, old boy?" The ghost nodded; though how he could nod when his head was off I don't know. Then the doctor got up and got a thread and needle, and sewed the ghost's head on, and pushed him gently out of the door, and told him never to show himself again. Nobody ever saw that ghost again, for the doctor had sewed his head on wrong side first, and he couldn't walk without running into the furniture, and of course he felt too much ashamed to show himself. This doctor was Mr. Travers's own grandfather, and Mr. Travers knows the story is true.

But I meant to tell you about the last time Mr. Martin came to our house. It was a week after I had scalped him; but I don't believe he would ever have come if father hadn't gone to see him, and urged him to overlook the rudeness of that unfortunate and thoughtless boy. When he did come, he was as smiling as anything; and he shook hands with me, and said, " Never mind, Bub, only don't do it again."

By-and-by, when Mr. Martin and Sue and Mr. Travers were sitting on the piazza, and I was playing with my new base-ball in the yard, Mr. Martin called out, " Pitch it over here ; give us a catch." So I tossed it over gently, and he pitched it back again, and said why didn't I throw it like a man, and not toss it like a girl. So I just sent him a swift ball—a regular daisy-cutter. I knew he couldn't catch it, but I expected he would dodge. He did try to dodge, but it hit him along-side of one eye, and knocked it out. You may think I am exaggelying, but I'm not. I saw that eye fly up against the side of the house, and then roll down the front steps to the front walk, where it stopped, and winked at me.

I turned, and ran out of the gate and down the street as hard as ever I could. I made up my mind that Mr. Martin was spoiled forever, and that the only thing for me to do was to make straight for the Spanish Main and be a pirate. I had often thought I would be a pirate, but now there was no help for it ; for a boy that had knocked out a gentle-man's eye could never be let to live in a Christian country. After a while I stopped to rest, and then I remembered that I wanted to take some provisions in a bundle, and a big knife to kill wolves. So I went back as soon as it was dark, and stole round to the back of the house, so I could get in the window and find the carving-knife and some cake. I was just getting in the window, when somebody put their arms around me, and said, "Dear little soul! was he almost frightened to death?" It was Sue, and I told her that I was going to be a pirate and wanted the carving-knife and some cake and she mustn't tell father and was Mr. Martin dead yet? So she told me that Mr. Martin's eye wasn't injured at all, and that he had put it in again, and gone home; and nobody would hurt me, and I needn't be a pirate if I didn't want to be.

It's perfectly dreadful for a man to be made like Mr. Martin, and I'll never come near him again. Sue says that he won't come back to the house, and if he does she'll send him away with something—I forget what it was—in his ear. Father hasn't heard about the eye yet, but if he does hear about it, there will be a dreadful scene, for he bought a new rattan cane yesterday. There ought to be a law to punish men that sell rattan canes to fathers, unless they haven't any children.

PLAYING CIRCUS.

The circus came through our town three weeks ago, and me and Tom McGinnis went to it. We didn't go together, for I went with father, and Tom helped the circus men water their horses, and they let him in for nothing. Father said that circuses were dreadfully demoralizing, unless they were mixed with wild animals, and that the reason why he took me to this particular circus was that there were elephants in it, and the elephant is a Scripture animal, Jimmy, and it cannot help but improve your mind to see him. I agreed with father. If my mind had to be improved, I thought going to the circus would be a good way to do it.

We had just an elegant time. I rode on the elephant, but it wasn't much fun for they wouldn't let me drive him. The trapeze was better than anything else, though the Central African Chariot Races and the Queen of the Arena, who rode on one foot, were gorgeous. The trapeze performances were done by the Patagonian Brothers, and you'd think every minute they were going to break their necks. Father said it was a most revolting sight and do sit down and keep still Jimmy or I can't see what's going on. I think father had a pretty good time, and improved his mind a good deal, for he was just as nice as he could be, and gave me a whole pint of pea-nuts.

Mr. Travers says that the Patagonian Brothers live on their trapezes, and never come down to the ground except when a performance is going to begin. They hook their legs around it at night, and sleep hanging with their heads down, just like the bats, and they take their meals and study their lessons sitting on the bar, without anything to lean against. I don't believe it; for how could they get their food brought up to them? and it's ridiculous to suppose that they have to study lessons. It grieves me very much to say so, but I am beginning to think that Mr. Travers doesn't always tell the truth. What did he mean by telling Sue the other night that he loved cats, and that her cat was perfectly beautiful, and then when she went into the other room he slung the cat out of the window, clear over into the asparagus bed, and said get out you brute? We cannot be too careful about always telling the truth, and never doing anything wrong.

Tom and I talked about the circus all the next day, and we agreed we'd have a circus of our own, and travel all over the country, and make heaps of money. We said we wouldn't let any of the other boys belong to it, but we

3

would do everything ourselves, except the elephants. So we began to practise in Mr. McGinnis's barn every afternoon after school. I was the Queen of the Arena, and dressed up in one of Sue's skirts, and won't she be mad when she finds that I cut the bottom off of it!—only I certainly meant to get her a new one with the very first money I made. I wore an old umbrella under the skirt, which made it stick out beautifully, and I know I should have looked splendid standing on Mr. McGinnis's old horse, only he was so slippery that I couldn't stand on him without falling off and sticking all the umbrella ribs into me.

Tom and I were the Madagascar Brothers, and we were going to do everything that the Patagonian Brothers did. We practised standing on each other's head hours at a time, and I did it pretty well, only Tom he slipped once when he was standing on my head, and sat down on it so hard that I don't much believe that my hair will ever grow any more.

The barn floor was most too hard to practise on, so last Saturday Tom said we'd go into the parlor, where there was a soft carpet, and we'd put some pillows on the floor besides. All Tom's folks had gone out, and there wasn't anybody in the house except the girl in the kitchen. So we went into the parlor, and put about a dozen pillows and a feather-bed on the floor. It was elegant fun turning

THE TRAPEZE PERFORMANCE,

somersaults backward from the top of the table; but I say it ought to be spelled summersets, though Sue says the other way is right.

We tried balancing things on our feet while we laid on our backs on the floor. Tom balanced the musical box for ever so long before it fell; but I don't think it was hurt much, for nothing except two or three little wheels were smashed. And I balanced the water-pitcher, and I shouldn't have broken it if Tom hadn't spoken to me at the wrong minute.

We were getting tired, when I thought how nice it would be to do the trapeze performance on the chandeliers. There was one in the front parlor and one in the back parlor, and I meant to swing on one of them, and let go and catch the other. I swung beautifully on the front parlor chandelier, when, just as I was going to let go of it, down it came with an awful crash, and that parlor was just filled with broken glass, and the gas began to smell dreadfully.

As it was about supper-time, and Tom's folks were expected home, I thought I would say good-bye to Tom, and not practise any more that day. So we shut the parlor doors, and I went home, wondering what would become of Tom, and whether I had done altogether right in practising with him in his parlor. There was an awful smell of gas in the house that night, and when Mr. McGinnis opened

the parlor door he found what was the matter.   He found
the cat too.   She was lying on the floor, just as dead as she
could be.

I'm going to see Mr. McGinnis to-day and tell him I
broke the chandelier.   I suppose he will tell father, and
then I shall wish that everybody had never been born ; but
I did break that chandelier, though I didn't mean to, and
I've got to tell about it.

MR. MARTIN'S LEG.

I had a dreadful time after that accident with Mr. Martin's eye. He wrote a letter to father and said that "the conduct of that atrocious young ruffian was such," and that he hoped he would never have a son like me. As soon as father said, "My son I want to see you up-stairs bring me my new rattan cane," I knew what was going to happen. I will draw some veils over the terrible scene, and will only say that for the next week I did not feel able to hold a pen unless I stood up all the time.

Last week I got a beautiful dog. Father had gone away for a few days and I heard mother say that she wished she had a nice little dog to stay in the house and drive robbers away. The very next day a lovely dog that didn't belong to anybody came into our yard and I made a dog-house for him out of a barrel, and got some beefsteak out of the closet for him, and got a cat for him to chase, and made him comfortable. He is part bull-dog, and his ears and tail are gone and he hasn't but one eye and he's lame in one of his hind-legs and the hair has been scalded off part of him, and he's just lovely. If you saw him after a cat you'd say he was a perfect beauty. Mother won't let me bring him into the house, and says she never saw such a horrid brute, but women haven't any taste about dogs anyway.

His name is Sitting Bull, though most of the time when he isn't chasing cats he's lying down. He knows pretty near everything. Some dogs know more than folks. Mr. Travers had a dog once that knew Chinese. Every time that dog heard a man speak Chinese he would lie down and howl and then he would get up and bite the man. You might talk English or French or Latin or German to him, and he wouldn't pay any attention to it, but just say three words in Chinese and he'd take a piece out of you. Mr. Travers says that once when he was a puppy a Chinaman tried to catch him for a stew; so whenever he heard anybody speak Chinese he remembered that time and went and bit the man to let him know that he didn't approve of the way Chinamen treated puppies. The dog never made a mistake but once. A man came to the house who had lost his pilate and couldn't speak plain, and the dog thought he was speaking Chinese and so he had his regular fit and bit the man worse than he had ever bit anybody before.

Sitting Bull don't know Chinese, but Mr. Travers says he's a "specialist in cats," which means that he knows the whole science of cats. The very first night I let him loose he chased a cat up the pear-tree and he sat under that tree and danced around it and howled all night. The neighbors next door threw most all their things at him but they couldn't discourage him. I had to tie him up after breakfast and let the cat get down and run away before I let him loose again, or he'd have barked all summer.

The only trouble with him is that he can't see very well and keeps running against things. If he starts to run out of the gate he is just as likely to run head first into the fence, and when he chases a cat round a corner he will sometimes mistake a stick of wood, or the lawn-mower for the cat and try to shake it to death. This was the way he came to get me into trouble with Mr. Martin.

He hadn't been at our house for so long (Mr. Martin I mean) that we all thought he never would come again. Father sometimes said that his friend Martin had been driven out of the house because my conduct was such and he expected I would separate him from all his friends. Of course I was sorry that father felt bad about it, but if I was his age I would have friends that were made more substantial than Mr. Martin is.

Night before last I was out in the back yard with Sitting Bull looking for a stray cat that sometimes comes around the house after dark and steals the strawberries and takes the apples out of the cellar. At least I suppose it is this particular cat that steals the apples, for the cook says a cat does it and we haven't any private cat of our own. After a while I saw the cat coming along by the side of the fence, looking wicked enough to steal anything and to tell stories about it afterwards. I was sitting on the ground holding Sitting Bull's head in my lap and telling him that I did wish he'd take to rat-hunting like Tom McGinnis's terrier, but no sooner had I seen the cat and whispered to Sitting Bull that she was in sight than he jumped up and went for her.

He chased her along the fence into the front yard where she made a dive under the front piazza. Sitting Bull came round the corner of the house just flying, and I close after him. It happened that Mr. Martin was at that identicular moment going up the steps of the piazza, and Sitting Bull mistaking one of his legs for the cat jumped for it and had it in his teeth before I could say a word.

When that dog once gets hold of a thing there is no use in reasoning with him, for he won't listen to anything. Mr. Martin howled and said, "Take him off my gracious the dog's mad" and I said, "Come here sir. Good dog. Leave him alone" but Sitting Bull hung on to the leg as if he was deaf and Mr. Martin hung on to the railing of the piazza and made twice as much noise as the dog. I didn't know whether I'd better run for the doctor or the police, but after shaking the leg for about a minute Sitting Bull gave it an awful pull and pulled it off just at the knee joint. When I saw the dog rushing round the yard with the leg in his mouth I ran into the house and told Sue and begged her to cut a hole in the wall and hide me behind the plastering where the police couldn't find me. When she went down to help Mr. Martin she saw him just going out of the yard on a wheelbarrow with a man wheeling him on a broad grin.

If he ever comes to this house again I'm going to run away. It turns out that his leg was made of cork and I suppose the rest of him is either cork or glass. Some day he'll drop apart on our piazza then the whole blame will be put on me.

OUR CONCERT.

THERE is one good thing about Sue, if she is a girl: she is real charitable, and is all the time getting people to give money to missionaries and things. She collected morna-hundred dollars from ever so many people last year, and sent it to a society, and her name was in all the papers as "Miss Susan Brown," the young lady that gave a hundred dollars to a noble cause and may others go and do like-wise.

About a month ago she began to get up a concert for a noble object. I forget what the object was, for Sue didn't make up her mind about it until a day or two be-fore the concert; but whatever it was, it didn't get much money.

Sue was to sing in the concert, and Mr. Travers was to sing, and father was to read something, and the Sunday-school was to sing, and the brass band was to play lots of things. Mr. Travers was real good about it, and attended to engaging the brass band, and getting the tickets printed.

We've got a first-rate band. You just ought to hear

it once. I'm going to join it some day, and play on the drum; that is, if they don't find out about the mistake I made with the music.

When Mr. Travers went to see the leader of the band to settle what music was to be played at the concert he let me go with him. The man was awfully polite, and he showed Mr. Travers great stacks of music for him to select from. After a while he proposed to go and see a man somewheres who played in the band, and they left me to wait until they came back.

I had nothing to do, so I looked at the music. The notes were all made with a pen and ink, and pretty bad they were. I should have been ashamed if I had made them. Just to prove that I could have done it better than the man who did do it, I took a pen and ink and tried it. I made beautiful notes, and as a great many of the pieces of music weren't half full of notes, I just filled in the places where there weren't any notes. I don't know how long Mr. Travers and the leader of the band were gone, but I was so busy that I did not miss them, and when I heard them coming I sat up as quiet as possible, and never said any-thing about what I had done, because we never should praise ourselves or seem to be proud of our own work.

Now I solemnly say that I never meant to do any harm. All I meant to do was to improve the music that the man

who wrote it had been too lazy to finish.   Why, in some of
those pieces of music there were places three or four inches
long without a single note, and you can't tell me that was
right.   But I sometimes think there is no use in trying to
help people as I tried to help our brass band.   People are
never grateful, and they always manage to blame a boy, no
matter how good he is.   I shall try, however, not to give
way to these feelings, but to keep on doing right no matter
what happens.

The next night we had the concert, or at any rate we
tried to have it.   The Town-hall was full of people, and
Sue said it did seem hard that so much money as the people had paid to come to the concert should all have to go
to charity when she really needed a new seal-skin coat.   The
performance was to begin with a song by Sue, and the band
was to play just like a piano while she was singing.   The
song was all about being so weary and longing so hard to
die, and Sue was singing it like anything, when all of a sudden the man with the big drum hit it a most awful bang,
and nearly frightened everybody to death.

People laughed out loud, and Sue could hardly go on
with her song.   But she took a fresh start, and got along
pretty well till the big drum broke out again, and the man
hammered away at it till the leader went and took his drum-
stick away from him.   The people just howled and yelled,

THERE WAS THE AWFULEST FIGHT YOU EVER SAW.

and Sue burst out crying and went right off the stage and longed to die in real earnest.

When things got a little bit quiet, and the man who played the drum had made it up with the leader, the band began to play something on its own account. It began all right, but it didn't finish the way it was meant to finish. First one player and then another would blow a loud note in the wrong place, and the leader would hammer on his music-stand, and the people would laugh themselves 'most sick. After a while the band came to a place where the trombones seemed to get crazy, and the leader just jumped up and knocked the trombone-player down with a big horn that he snatched from another man. Then somebody hit the leader with a cornet and knocked him into the big drum, and there was the awfullest fight you ever saw till somebody turned out the gas.

There wasn't any more concert that night, and the people all got their money back, and now Mr. Travers and the leader of the band have offered a reward for " the person who maliciously altered the music "—that's what the notice says. But I wasn't malicious, and I do hope nobody will find out I did it, though I mean to tell father about it as soon as he gets over having his nose pretty near broke by trying to interfere between the trombone-player and the man with the French horn.

4

OUR BABY.

Mr. Martin has gone away. He's gone to Europe or Hartford or some such place. Anyway I hope we'll never see him again. The expressman says that part of him went in the stage and part of him was sent in a box by express, but I don't know whether it is true or not.

I never could see the use of babies. We have one at our house that belongs to mother and she thinks everything of it. I can't see anything wonderful about it. All it can do is to cry and pull hair and kick. It hasn't half the sense of my dog, and it can't even chase a cat. Mother and Sue wouldn't have a dog in the house, but they are always going on about the baby and saying "ain't it perfectly sweet!" Why, I wouldn't change Sitting Bull for a dozen babies, or at least I wouldn't change him if I had him. After the time he bit Mr. Martin's leg father said "that brute sha'n't stay here another day." I don't know what became of him, but the next morning he was gone and I have never seen him since. I have had great sorrows though people think I'm only a boy.

The worst thing about a baby is that you're expected to take care of him and then you get scolded afterwards. Folks say, " Here, Jimmy! just hold the baby a minute, that's a good boy," and then as soon as you have got it they say, " Don't do that my goodness gracious the boy will kill the child hold it up straight you good-for-nothing little wretch." It is pretty hard to do your best and then be scolded for it, but that's the way boys are treated. Perhaps after I'm dead folks will wish they had done differently.

Last Saturday mother and Sue went out to make calls and told me to stay home and take care of the baby. There was a base-ball match but what did they care? They didn't want to go to it and so it made no difference whether I went to it or not. They said they would be gone only a little while, and that if the baby waked up I was to play with it and keep it from crying and be sure you don't let it swallow any pins. Of course I had to do it. The baby was sound asleep when they went out, so I left it just for a few minutes while I went to see if there was any pie in the pantry. If I was a woman I wouldn't be so dreadfully suspicious as to keep everything locked up. When I got back up-stairs again the baby was awake and was howling like he was full of pins; so I gave him the first thing that came handy to keep him quiet. It happened to be a bottle of French polish with a sponge in it on the end of a wire that Sue uses to black her shoes, because girls are too lazy to use a regular blacking-brush.

The baby stopped crying as soon as I gave him the bottle and I sat down to read. The next time I looked at him he'd got out the sponge and about half his face was jet-black. This was a nice fix, for I knew nothing could get the black off his face, and when mother came home she would say the baby was spoiled and I had done it.

Now I think an all black baby is ever so much more stylish than an all white baby, and when I saw the baby was part black I made up my mind that if I blacked it all over it would be worth more than it ever had been and perhaps mother would be ever so much pleased. So I hurried up and gave it a good coat of black. You should have seen how that baby shined! The polish dried just as soon as it was put on, and I had just time to get the baby dressed again when mother and Sue came in.

I wouldn't lower myself to repeat their unkind language. When you've been called a murdering little villain and an unnatural son it will wrinkle in your heart for ages. After what they said to me I didn't even seem to mind about father but went up-stairs with him almost as if I was going to church or something that wouldn't hurt much.

The baby is beautiful and shiny, though the doctor says it will wear off in a few years. Nobody shows any gratitude for all the trouble I took, and I can tell you it isn't easy to black a baby without getting it into his eyes and hair. I sometimes think that it is hardly worth while to live in this cold and unfeeling world.

OUR SNOW MAN.

I do love snow. There isn't anything except a bull-terrier that is as beautiful as snow. Mr. Travers says that seven hundred men once wrote a poem called "Beautiful Snow," and that even then, though they were all big strong men, they couldn't find words enough to tell how beautiful it was.

There are some people who like snow, and some who don't. It's very curious, but that's the way it is about almost everything. There are the Eskimos who live up North where there isn't anything but snow, and where there are no schools nor any errands, and they haven't anything to do but to go fishing and skating and hunting, and sliding down hill all day. Well, the Eskimos don't like it, for people who have been there and seen them say they are dreadfully dissatisfied. A nice set the Eskimos must be! I wonder what would satisfy them. I don't suppose it's any use trying to find out, for father says there's no limit to the unreasonableness of some people.

We ought always to be satisfied and contented with our

condition and the things we have. I'm always contented when I have what I want, though of course nobody can expect a person to be contented when things don't satisfy him. Sue is real contented, too, for she's got the greatest amount of new clothes, and she's going to be married very soon. I think it's about time she was, and most everybody else thinks so too, for I've heard them say so; and they've said so more than ever since we made the snow man.

You see, it was the day before Christmas, and there had been a beautiful snow-storm. All of us boys were sliding down hill, when somebody said, "Let's make a snow man." Everybody seemed to think the idea was a good one, and we made up our minds to build the biggest snow man that ever was, just for Christmas. The snow was about a foot thick, and just hard enough to cut into slabs; so we got a shovel and went to work. We built the biggest snow man I ever heard of. We made him hollow, and Tom McGinnis stood inside of him and helped build while the rest of us worked on the outside. Just as fast as we got a slab of snow in the right place we poured water on it so that it would freeze right away. We made the outside of the man about three feet thick, and he was so tall that Tom McGinnis had to keep climbing up inside of him to help build.

Tom came near getting into a dreadful scrape, for we

forgot to leave a hole for him to get out of, and when the
man was done, and frozen as hard as a rock, Tom found
that he was shut up as tight as if he was in prison. Didn't
he howl, though, and beg us to let him out! I told him
that he would be very foolish not to stay in the man all
night, for he would be as warm as the Eskimos are in
their snow huts, and there would be such fun when people
couldn't find him anywhere. But Tom wasn't satisfied;
he began to talk some silly nonsense about wanting his
supper. The idea of anybody talking about such a little
thing as supper when they had such a chance to make a
big stir as that. Tom always was an obstinate sort of fellow, and he would insist upon coming out, so we got a
hatchet and chopped a hole in the back of the man and let
him out.

The snow man was quite handsome, and we made him
have a long beak, like a bird, so that people would be astonished when they saw him. It was that beak that made
me think about the Egyptian gods that had heads like
hawks and other birds and animals, and must have frightened people dreadfully when they suddenly met them near
graveyards or in lonesome roads.

One of those Egyptian gods was made of stone, and was
about as high as the top of a house. He was called Memnon, and every morning at sunrise he used to sing out with

WE BUILT THE BIGGEST SNOW MAN I EVER HEARD OF.

a loud voice, just as the steam-whistle at Mr. Thompson's mill blows every morning at sunrise to wake people up. The Egyptians thought that Memnon was something wonderful, but it has been found out, since the Egyptians died, that a priest used to hide himself somewhere inside of Memnon, and made all the noise.

Looking at the snow man and thinking about the Egyptian gods, I thought it wouldn't be a bad idea to hide inside of him and say things whenever people went by. It would be a new way of celebrating Christmas, too. They would be awfully astonished to hear a snow man talk. I might even make him sing a carol, and then he'd be a sort of Christian Memnon, and nobody would think I had anything to do with it.

That evening when the moon got up—it was a beautiful moonlight night—I slipped out quietly and went up to the hill where the snow man was, and hid inside of him. I knew Mr. Travers and Sue were out sleigh-riding, and they hadn't asked me to go, though there was lots of room, and I meant to say something to them when they drove by the snow man that would make Sue wish she had been a little more considerate.

Presently I heard bells and looked out and saw a sleigh coming up the hill. I was sure it was Mr. Travers and Sue; so I made ready for them. The sleigh came up the hill very slow, and when it was nearly opposite to me I said, in a solemn voice, " Susan, you ought to have been married long ago." You see, I knew that would please Mr. Travers ; and it was true, too.

She gave a shriek, and said, " Oh, what's that ?"

" We'll soon see," said a man's voice that didn't sound a bit like Mr. Travers's. " There's somebody round here that's spoiling for a thrashing."

The man came right up to the snow man, and saw my legs through the hole, and got hold of one of them and began to pull. I didn't know it, but the boys had undermined the snow man on one side, and as soon as the man began to pull, over went the snow man and me right into the sleigh, and the woman screamed again, and the horse ran away and pitched us out, and—

But I don't want to tell the rest of it, only father said that I must be taught not to insult respectable ladies like Miss Susan White, who is fifty years old, by telling them it is time they were married.

ART.

Our town has been very lively this winter. First we had two circuses, and then we had the small-pox, and now we've got a course of lectures. A course of lectures is six men, and you can go to sleep while they're talking, if you want to, and you'd better do it unless they are missionaries with real idols or a magic lantern. I always go to sleep before the lectures are through, but I heard a good deal of one of them that was all about art.

Art is almost as useful as history or arithmetic, and we ought all to learn it, so that we can make beautiful things and elevate our minds. Art is done with mud in the first place. The art man takes a large chunk of mud and squeezes it until it is like a beautiful man or woman, or wild bull, and then he takes a marble gravestone and cuts it with a chisel until it is exactly like the piece of mud. If you want a solid photograph of yourself made out of marble, the art man covers your face with mud, and when it gets hard he takes it off, and the inside of it is just like a

mould, so that he can fill it full of melted marble which
will be an exact photograph of you as soon as it gets cool.

This is what one of the men who belong to the course of
lectures told us. He said he would have shown us exactly
how to do art, and would have made a beautiful portrait of
a friend of his, named Vee Nuss, right on the stage before
our eyes, only he couldn't get the right kind of mud. I
believed him then, but I don't believe him now. A man
who will contrive to get an innocent boy into a terrible
scrape isn't above telling what isn't true. He could have
got mud if he'd wanted it, for there was mornamillion
tons of it in the street, and it's my belief that he couldn't
have made anything beautiful if he'd had mud a foot deep
on the stage.

As I said, I believed everything the man said, and when
the lecture was over, and father said, "I do hope Jimmy
you've got some benefit from the lecture this time;" and
Sue said, "A great deal of benefit that boy will ever get
unless he gets it with a good big switch don't I wish I was
his father O! I'd let him know," I made up my mind that
I would do some art the very next day, and show people
that I could get lots of benefit if I wanted to.

I have spoken about our baby a good many times. It's
no good to anybody, and I call it a failure. It's a year and
three months old now, and it can't talk or walk, and as for

THE MOMENT THEY SAW THE BABY THEY SAID THE MOST DREADFUL THINGS.

reading or writing, you might as well expect it to play base-ball. I always knew how to read and write, and there must be something the matter with this baby, or it would know more.

Last Monday mother and Sue went out to make calls, and left me to take care of the baby. They had done that before, and the baby had got me into a scrape, so I didn't want to be exposed to its temptations; but the more I begged them not to leave me, the more they would do it, and mother said, "I know you'll stay and be a good boy while we go and make those horrid calls," and Sue said, "I'd better or I'd get what I wouldn't like."

After they'd gone I tried to think what I could do to please them, and make everybody around me better and happier. After a while I thought that it would be just the thing to do some art and make a marble photograph of the baby, for that would show everybody that I had got some benefit from the lectures, and the photograph of the baby would delight mother and Sue.

I took mother's fruit-basket and filled it with mud out of the back yard. It was nice thick mud, and it would stay in any shape that you squeezed it into, so that it was just the thing to do art with. I laid the baby on its back on the bed, and covered its face all over with the mud about two inches thick. A fellow who didn't know anything about

5

art might have killed the baby, for if you cover a baby's mouth and nose with mud it can't breathe, which is very unhealthy, but I left its nose so it could breathe, and intended to put an extra piece of mud over that part of the mould after it was dry. Of course the baby howled all it could, and it would have kicked dreadfully, only I fastened its arms and legs with a shawl-strap so that it couldn't do itself any harm.

The mud wasn't half dry when mother and Sue and father came in, for he met them at the front gate. They all came up-stairs, and the moment they saw the baby they said the most dreadful things to me without waiting for me to explain. I did manage to explain a little through the closet door while father was looking for his rattan cane, but it didn't do the least good.

I don't want to hear any more about art or to see any more lectures. There is nothing so ungrateful as people, and if I did do what wasn't just what people wanted, they might have remembered that I meant well, and only wanted to please them and elevate their minds.

AN AWFUL SCENE.

I HAVE the same old, old story to tell. My conduct has been such again—at any rate, that's what father says; and I've had to go up-stairs with him, and I needn't explain what that means. It seems very hard, for I'd tried to do my very best, and I'd heard Sue say, "That boy hasn't misbehaved for two days good gracious I wonder what can be the matter with him." There's a fatal litty about it, I'm sure. Poor father! I must give him an awful lot of trouble, and I know he's had to get two new bamboo canes this winter just because I've done so wrong, though I never meant to do it.

It happened on account of coasting. We've got a magnificent hill. The road runs straight down the middle of it, and all you have to do is to keep on the road. There's a fence on one side, and if you run into it something has got to break. John Kruger, who is a stupid sort of a fellow, ran into it last week head-first, and smashed three pickets, and everybody said it was a mercy he hit it with his head, or he might have broken some of his bones and

hurt himself.   There isn't any fence on the other side, but
if you run off the road on that side you'll go down the side
of a hill that's steeper than the roof of the Episcopal church,
and about a mile long, with a brook full of stones down at
the bottom.

The other night Mr. Travers said—   But I forgot to say
that Mr. Martin is back again, and coming to our house
worse than ever.   He was there, and Mr. Travers and Sue,
all sitting in the parlor, where I was behaving, and trying
to make things pleasant, when Mr. Travers said, "It's a
bright moonlight night let's all go out and coast."   Sue
said, "Oh that would be lovely Jimmy get your sled."   I
didn't encourage them, and I told father so, but he wouldn't
admit that Mr. Travers or Sue or Mr. Martin or anybody
could do anything wrong.   What I said was, " I don't want
to go coasting.   It's cold and I don't feel very well, and I
think we ought all to go to bed early so we can wake up
real sweet and good-tempered."   But Sue just said, " Don't
you preach Jimmy if you're lazy just say so and Mr. Travers
will take us out."   Then Mr. Martin he must put in and
say, " Perhaps the boy's afraid don't tease him he ought to
be in bed anyhow."   Now I wasn't going to stand this, so
I said, "Come on.   I wanted to go all the time, but I
thought it would be best for old people to stay at home,
and that's why I didn't encourage you."   So I got out my

double-ripper, and we all went out on the hill and started down.

I sat in front to steer, and Sue sat right behind me, and Mr. Travers sat behind her to hold her on, and Mr. Martin sat behind him. We went splendidly, only the dry snow flew so that I couldn't see anything, and that's why we got off the road and on to the side hill before I knew it.

The hill was just one glare of ice, and the minute we struck the ice the sled started away like a hurricane. I had just time to hear Mr. Martin say, "Boy mind what you're about or I'll get off," when she struck something—I don't know what—and everybody was pitched into the air, and began sliding on the ice without anything to help them, except me. I caught on a bare piece of rock, and stopped myself. I could see Sue sitting up straight, and sliding like a streak of lightning, and crying, "Jimmy father Charles Mr. Martin O my help me." Mr. Travers was on his stomach, about a rod behind her, and gaining a little on her, and Mr. Martin was on his back, coming down head-first, and beating them both. All of a sudden he began to go to pieces. Part of him would slide off one way, and then another part would try its luck by itself. I can tell you it was an awful and surreptitious sight. They all reached the bottom after a while, and when I saw they were not killed, I tried it myself, and landed all right. Sue was

sitting still, and mourning, and saying, " My goodness gracious I shall never be able to walk again my comb is
broken and that boy isn't fit to live." Mr. Travers wasn't
hurt very much, and he fixed himself all right with some
pins I gave him, and his handkerchief; but his overcoat
looked as if he'd stolen it from a scarecrow. When he had
comforted Sue a little (and I must say some people are perfectly sickening the way they go on), he and I collected Mr.
Martin—all except his teeth—and helped put him together,
only I got his leg on wrong side first, and then we helped
him home.

This was why father said that my conduct was such, and
that his friend Martin didn't seem to be able to come into
his house without being insulted and injured by me. I
never insulted him. It isn't my fault if he can't slide down
a hill without coming apart. However, I've had my last
suffering on account of him. The next time he comes apart
where I am I shall not wait to be punished for it, but shall
start straight for the North-pole, and if I discover it the
British government will pay me mornamillion dollars. I'm
able to sit down this morning, but my spirits are crushed,
and I shall never enjoy life any more.

SCREW-HEADS.

I'M in an awful situation that a boy by the name of Bellew got me into. He is one of the boys that writes stories and makes pictures for HARPER'S YOUNG PEOPLE, and I think people ought to know what kind of a boy he is. A little while ago he had a story in the YOUNG PEOPLE about imitation screw-heads, and how he used to make them, and what fun he had pasting them on his aunt's bureau. I thought it was a very nice story, and I got some tin-foil and made a whole lot of screw-heads, and last Saturday I thought I'd have some fun with them.

Father has a dreadfully ugly old chair in his study, that General Washington brought over with him in the *May-flower*, and Mr. Travers says it is stiffer and uglier than any of the Pilgrim fathers. But father thinks everything of that chair, and never lets anybody sit in it except the minister. I took a piece of soap, just as that Bellew used to, and if his name is Billy why don't he learn how to spell it that's what I'd like to know, and made what looked like a tremendous crack in the chair. Then I pasted the screw-heads on the chair, and it looked exactly as if somebody had broken it and tried to mend it.

I couldn't help laughing all day when I thought how as-

tonished father would be when he saw his chair all full of
screws, and how he would laugh when he found out it was
all a joke. As soon as he came home I asked him to please
come into the study, and showed him the chair and said

" Father I cannot tell a lie I did it but I won't do it any more."

Father looked as if he had seen some disgusting ghosts, and I was really frightened, so I hurried up and said, " It's all right father, it's only a joke look here they all come off," and rubbed off the screw-heads and the soap with my hand-kerchief, and expected to see him burst out laughing, just as Bellew's aunt used to burst, but instead of laughing he said, " My son this trifling with sacred things must be stopped," with which remark he took off his slipper, and then— But I haven't the heart to say what he did. Mr. Travers has made some pictures about it, and perhaps people will understand what I have suffered.

I think that boy Bellew ought to be punished for getting people into scrapes. I'd just like to have him come out behind our barn with me for a few minutes. That is, I would, only I never expect to take any interest in anything any more. My heart is broken and a new chocolate cigar that was in my pocket during the awful scene.

I've got an elegant wasps' nest with young wasps in it that will hatch out in the spring, and I'll change it for a bull-terrier or a shot-gun or a rattlesnake in a cage that rattles good with any boy that will send me one.

MY MONKEY.

THERE never was such luck. I've always thought that I'd rather have a monkey than be a million heir. There is nothing that could be half so splendid as a real live monkey, but of course I knew that I never could have one until I should grow up and go to sea and bring home monkeys and parrots and shawls to mother just as sailors always do. But I've actually got a monkey and if you don't believe it just look at these pictures of him that Mr. Travers made for me.

It was Mr. Travers that got the monkey for me. One day there came a woman with an organ and a monkey into our yard.

She was an Italian, but she could speak a sort of English and she said that the "murderin' spalpeen of a monkey was just wearing the life of her out." So says Mr. Travers "What will you take for him?" and says she "It's five dollars I'd be after selling him for, and may good-luck go wid ye!"

What did Mr. Travers do but give her the money and

hand the monkey to me, saying, "Here, Jimmy! take him
and be happy." Wasn't I just happy though?

Jocko—that's the monkey's name—is the loveliest monkey that ever lived. I hadn't had him an hour when he got out of my arms and was on the supper-table before I could get him. The table was all set and Bridget was just going to ring the bell, but the monkey didn't wait for her.

To see him eating the chicken salad was just wonderful. He finished the whole dish in about two minutes, and was washing it down with the oil out of the salad - bottle when I caught him. Mother was awfully good about it and only said, " Poor little beast he must be half starved

Susan how much he reminds me of your brother." A good mother is as good a thing as a boy deserves, no matter how good he is.

The salad someway did not seem to agree with Jocko for he was dreadfully sick that night. You should have seen how limp he was, just like a girl that has fainted away and her young man is trying to lift her up. Mother doctored him. She gave him castor-oil as if he was her own son, and wrapped him up in a blanket and put a mustard plaster on his stomach and soaked the end of his tail in warm water.   He was all right the next day and was real grate-

ful.   I know he was grateful because he showed it by trying to do good to others, at any rate to the cat.   Our cat wouldn't speak to him at first, but he coaxed her with milk, just as he had seen me do and finally caught her.   It must have been dreadfully aggravoking to the cat, for instead of letting her have the milk he insisted that she was sick and must have medicine.   So he took Bridget's bottle of hair-oil and a big spoon and gave the cat such a dose.   When I caught him and made him let the cat go there were about six table-spoonfuls of oil missing.   Mr. Travers said it was a good thing for it would improve the cat's voice and make her yowl smoother, and that he had felt for a long time that she needed to be oiled.   Mother said that the monkey was cruel and it was a shame but I know that he meant to be kind. He knew the oil mother gave him had done him good, and he wanted to do the cat good. I know just how he felt, for I've been blamed many a time for trying to do good, and I can tell you it always hurt my feelings.

The monkey was in the kitchen while Bridget was getting dinner yesterday and he watched her broil the steak as if he was meaning to learn to cook and help her in her work, he's that kind and thoughtful. The cat was out-doors, but two of her kittens were in the kitchen, and they were not old enough to be afraid of the monkey. When dinner was served Bridget went up-stairs and by-and-by mother

says " What's that dreadful smell sure's you're alive Susan
the baby has fallen into the fire." Everybody jumped up
and ran up-stairs, all but me, for I knew Jocko was in the
kitchen and I was afraid it was he that was burning. When
I got into the kitchen there was that lovely monkey broil-
ing one of the kittens on the gridiron just as he had seen
Bridget broil the steak. The kitten's fur was singeing and

she was mewing, and
the other kitten was
sitting up on the floor
licking her chops and
enjoying it and Jocko
was on his hind-legs as
solemn and busy as an
owl. I snatched the
gridiron away from him
and took the kitten off
before she was burned
any except her fur, and
when mother and Susan came down-stairs they couldn't
understand what it was that had been burning.

This is all the monkey has done since I got him day
before yesterday. Father has been away for a week but is
coming back in a few days, and won't he be delighted when
he finds a monkey in the house ?

THE END OF MY MONKEY.

I haven't any monkey now, and I don't care what becomes of me. His loss was an awful blow, and I never expect to recover from it. I am a crushed boy, and when the grown folks find what their conduct has done to me, they will wish they had done differently.

It was on a Tuesday that I got the monkey, and by Thursday everybody began to treat him coldly. It began with my littlest sister. Jocko took her doll away, and climbed up to the top of the door with it, where he sat and pulled it to pieces, and tried its clothes on, only they wouldn't fit him, while sister, who is nothing but a little girl, stood and howled as if she was being killed. This made mother begin to dislike the monkey, and she said that if his conduct was such, he couldn't stay in her house. I call this unkind, for the monkey was invited into the house, and I've been told we must bear with visitors.

A little while afterwards, while mother was talking to Susan on the front piazza, she heard the sewing-machine up-stairs, and said, "Well I never that cook has the im-

6

pudence to be sewing on my machine without ever asking leave." So she ran up-stairs, and found that Jocko was working the machine like mad. He'd taken Sue's gown and father's black coat and a lot of stockings, and shoved them all under the needle, and was sewing them all together. Mother boxed his ears, and then she and Sue sat down and worked all the morning trying to unsew the things with the scissors.

They had to give it up after a while, and the things are sewed together yet, like a man and wife, which no man can put asunder. All this made my mother more cool towards the monkey than ever, and I heard her call him a nasty little beast.

The next day was Sunday, and as Sue was sitting in the hall waiting for mother to go to church with her. Jocko gets up on her chair, and pulls the feathers out of her bonnet. He thought he was doing right, for he had seen the cook pulling the feathers off of the chickens, but Sue called him dreadful names, and said that when father came home, either she or that monkey would leave the house.

Father came home early Monday, and seemed quite pleased with the monkey. He said it was an interesting study, and he told Susan that he hoped that she would be contented with fewer beaux, now that there was a monkey constantly in the house. In a little while father caught Jocko lathering himself with the mucilage brush, and with a kitchen knife all ready to shave himself. He just laughed at the monkey, and told me to take good care of him, and not let him hurt himself. Of course I was dreadfully pleased to find that father liked Jocko, and I knew it was because he was a man, and had more sense than girls. But I was only deceiving myself and leaning on a broken weed. That very evening when father went into his study after

supper he found Jocko on his desk. He had torn all his papers to pieces, except a splendid new map, and that he was covering with ink, and making believe that he was writing a President's Message about the Panama Canal. Father was just raging. He took Jocko by the scruff of the neck, locked him in the closet, and sent him away by express the next morning to a man in the city, with orders to sell him.

The expressman afterwards told Mr. Travers that the

monkey pretty nearly killed everybody on the train, for he got hold of the signal-cord and pulled it, and the engineer thought it was the conductor, and stopped the train, and another train just behind it came within an inch of running into it and smashing it to pieces. Jocko did the same

thing three times before they found out what was the matter, and tied him up so that he couldn't reach the cord. Oh, he was just beautiful! But I shall never see him again, and Mr. Travers says that it's all right, and that I'm monkey enough for one house. That's because

Sue has been saying things against the monkey to him; but never mind.

First my dog went, and now my monkey has gone. It

seems as if everything that is beautiful must disappear.
Very likely I shall go next, and when I am gone, let them
find the dog and the monkey, and bury us together.

THE OLD, OLD STORY.

WE'VE had a most awful time in our house. There have been ever so many robberies in town, and everybody has been almost afraid to go to bed.

The robbers broke into old Dr. Smith's house one night. Dr. Smith is one of those doctors that don't give any medicine 'except cold water, and he heard the robbers, and came down-stairs in his nigown, with a big umbrella in his hand, and said, "If you don't leave this minute, I'll shoot you." And the robbers they said, "Oh no! that umbrella isn't loaded;" and they took him and tied his hands and feet, and put a mustard-plaster over his mouth, so that he couldn't yell, and then they filled the wash-tub with water, and made him sit down in it, and told him that now he'd know how it was himself, and went away and left him, and he nearly froze to death before morning.

Father wasn't a bit afraid of the robbers, but he said he'd fix something so that he would wake up if they got in the house. So he put a coal-scuttle full of coal about half-way up the stairs, and tied a string across the upper hall just at the head of the stairs. He said that if a robber tried to come up-stairs he would upset the coal-scuttle, and make a tremendous noise, and that if he did happen not to upset it, he would certainly fall over the string at the top of the stairs. He told us that if we heard the coal-scuttle go off in the night, Sue and mother and I were to open the windows and scream, while he got up and shot the robber.

The first night, after father had fixed everything nicely for the robbers, he went to bed, and then mother told him that she had forgotten to lock the back door. So father he said, " Why can't women sometimes remember something," and he got up and started to go down-stairs in the dark. He forgot all about the string, and fell over it with an awful crash, and then began to fall down-stairs. When he got half-way down he met the coal-scuttle, and that went down the rest of the way with him, and you never in your life heard anything like the noise the two of them made. We opened our windows, and cried murder and fire and thieves, and some men that were going by rushed in and picked father up, and would have taken him off to jail, he was that dreadfully black, if I hadn't told them who he was.

But this was not the awful time that I mentioned when I began to write, and if I don't begin to tell you about it, I sha'n't have any room left on my paper. Mother gave a dinner-party last Thursday. There were ten ladies and

WASN'T THERE A CIRCUS IN THAT DINING-ROOM!

twelve gentlemen, and one of them was that dreadful Mr. Martin with the cork leg, and other improvements, as Mr. Travers calls them. Mother told me not to let her see me in the dining-room, or she'd let me know; and I meant to mind, only I forgot, and went into the dining-room, just to look at the table, a few minutes before dinner.

I was looking at the raw oysters, when Jane—that's the girl that waits on the table—said, "Run, Master Jimmy; here's your mother coming." Now I hadn't time enough to run, so I just dived under the table, and thought I'd stay there for a minute or two, until mother went out of the room again.

It wasn't only mother that came in, but the whole company, and they sat down to dinner without giving me any chance to get out. I tell you, it was a dreadful situation. I had only room enough to sit still, and nearly every time I moved I hit somebody's foot. Once I tried to turn around, and while I was doing it I hit my head against the table so hard that I thought I had upset something, and was sure that people would know I was there. But fortunately everybody thought that somebody else had joggled, so I escaped for that time.

It was awfully tiresome waiting for those people to get through dinner. It seemed as if they could never eat enough, and when they were not eating, they were all talking at once. It taught me a lesson against gluttony, and nobody will ever find me sitting for hours and hours at the dinner-table. Finally I made up my mind that I must have some amusement, and as Mr. Martin's cork-leg was close by me, I thought I would have some fun with that.

There was a big darning-needle in my pocket, that I kept there in case I should want to use it for anything. I happened to think that Mr. Martin couldn't feel anything that was done to his cork-leg, and that it would be great fun to drive the darning-needle into it, and leave the end sticking out, so that people who didn't know that his leg was cork would see it, and think that he was suffering dreadfully, only he didn't know it. So I got out the needle, and jammed it into his leg with both hands, so that it would go in good and deep.

Mr. Martin gave a yell that made my hair run cold, and sprang up, and nearly upset the table, and fell over his chair backward, and wasn't there a circus in that dining-room! I had made a mistake about the leg, and run the needle into his real one.

I was dragged out from under the table, and— But I needn't say what happened to me after that. It was "the old, old story," as Sue says when she sings a foolish song about getting up at five o'clock in the morning—as if she'd ever been awake at that time in her whole life!

BEE-HUNTING.

THE more I see of this world the hollower I find every-body. I don't mean that people haven't got their insides in them, but they are so dreadfully ungrateful. No matter how kind and thoughtful any one may be, they never give him any credit for it. They will pretend to love you and call you "Dear Jimmy what a fine manly boy come here and kiss me," and then half an hour afterwards they'll say "Where's that little wretch let me just get hold of him O! I'll let him know." Deceit and ingratitude are the monster vices of the age and they are rolling over our beloved land like the flood. (I got part of that elegant language from the temperance lecturer last week, but I improved it a good deal.)

There is Aunt Eliza. The uncle that belonged to her died two years ago, and she's awfully rich. She comes to see us sometimes with Harry—that's her boy, a little fellow six years old—and you ought to see how mother and Sue wait on her and how pleasant father is when she's in the room. Now she always said that she loved me like her own son. She'd say to father, " How I envy you that noble boy what a comfort he must be to you," and father would say " Yes he has some charming qualities " and look as if he hadn't laid onto me with his cane that very morning and told me that my conduct was such. You'll hardly believe that just because I did the very best I could and saved her precious Harry from an apple grave, Aunt Eliza says I'm a young Cain and knows I'll come to the gallows.

She came to see us last Friday, and on Saturday I was going bee-hunting. I read all about it in a book. You take an axe and go out-doors and follow a bee, and after a while the bee takes you to a hollow tree full of honey and you cut the tree down and carry the honey home in thirty pails and sell it for ever so much. I and Tom McGinnis were going and Aunt Eliza says " O take Harry with you the dear child would enjoy it so much." Of course no fellow that's twelve years old wants a little chap like that tagging after him but mother spoke up and said that I'd be delighted to take Harry, and so I couldn't help myself.

We stopped in the wood-shed and borrowed father's axe and then we found a bee. The bee wouldn't fly on before us in a straight line but kept lighting on everything, and once he lit on Tom's hand and stung him good. However we chased the bee lively and by-and-by he started for his tree and we ran after him. We had just got to the old dead apple-tree in the pasture when we lost the bee and we all agreed that his nest must be in the tree. It's an awfully big old tree, and it's all rotted away on one side so that it stands as if it was ready to fall over any minute.

Nothing would satisfy Harry but to climb that tree. We told him he'd better let a bigger fellow do it but he wouldn't listen to reason. So we gave him a boost and he climbed up to where the tree forked and then he stood up and began to say something when he disappeared. We thought he had fallen out of the tree and we ran round to the other side to pick him up but he wasn't there. Tom said it was witches but I knew he must be somewhere so I climbed up the tree and looked.

He had slipped down into the hollow of the tree and was wedged in tight. I could just reach his hair but it was so short that I couldn't get a good hold so as to pull him out. Wasn't he scared though! He howled and said "O take me out I shall die," and Tom wanted to run for the doctor.

I told Harry to be patient and I'd get him out. So I slid down the tree and told Tom that the only thing to do was to cut the tree down and then open it and take Harry out. It was such a rotten tree I knew it would come down easy. So we took turns chopping, and the fellow who wasn't chopping kept encouraging Harry by telling him that the tree was 'most ready to fall. After working an hour

the tree began to stagger and presently down she came
with an awful crush and burst into a million pieces.

Tom and I said Hurray! and then we poked round in
the dust till we found Harry. He was all over red dust
and was almost choked, but he was awfully mad. Just
because some of his ribs were broke—so the doctor said—
he forget all Tom and I had done for him. I shouldn't
have minded that much, because you don't expect much
from little boys, but I did think his mother would have
been grateful when we brought him home and told her
what we had done. Then I found what all her professions
were worth. She called father and told him that I and the
other miscurrent had murdered her boy. Tom was so
frightened at the awful name she called him that he ran
home, and father told me I could come right up-stairs with
him.

They couldn't have treated me worse if I'd let Harry
stay in the tree and starve to death. I almost wish I had
done it. It does seem as if the more good a boy does the
more the grown folks pitch into him. The moment Sue
is married to Mr. Travers I mean to go and live with him.
He never scolds, and always says that Susan's brother is as
dear to him as his own, though he hasn't got any.

PROMPT OBEDIENCE.

I HAVEN'T been able to write anything for some time. I don't mean that there has been anything the matter with my fingers so that I couldn't hold a pen, but I haven't had the heart to write of my troubles. Besides, I have been locked up for a whole week in the spare bedroom on bread and water, and just a little hash or something like that, except when Sue used to smuggle in cake and pie and such things, and I haven't had any penanink. I was going to write a novel while I was locked up by pricking my finger and writing in blood with a pin on my shirt; but you can't write hardly anything that way, and I don't believe all those stories of conspirators who wrote dreadful promises to do all sorts of things in their blood. Before I could write two little words my finger stopped bleeding, and I wasn't going to keep on pricking myself every few minutes; besides, it won't do to use all your blood up that way. There was once a boy who cut himself awful in the leg with a knife, and he bled to death for five or six hours, and

7

when he got through he wasn't any thicker than a news-paper, and rattled when his friends picked him up just like the morning paper does when father turns it inside out. Mr. Travers told me about him, and said this was a warning against bleeding to death.

Of course you'll say I must have been doing something dreadfully wrong, but I don't think I have; and even if I had, I'll leave it to anybody if Aunt Eliza isn't enough to provoke a whole company of saints. The truth is, I got into trouble this time just through obeying promptly as soon as I was spoken to. I'd like to know if that was anything wrong. Oh, I'm not a bit sulky, and I am always ready to admit I've done wrong when I really have; but this time I tried to do my very best and obey my dear mother promptly, and the consequence was that I was shut up for a week, besides other things too painful to mention. This world is a fleeting show, as our minister says, and I sometimes feel that it isn't worth the price of admission.

Aunt Eliza is one of those women that always know everything, and know that nobody else knows anything, particularly us men. She was visiting us, and finding fault with everybody, and constantly saying that men were a nuisance in a house and why didn't mother make father mend chairs and whitewash the ceiling and what do you let that great lazy boy waste all his time for? There was a

little spot in the roof where it leaked when it rained, and
Aunt Eliza said to father, "Why don't you have energy
enough to get up on the roof and see where that leak is
I would if I was a man thank goodness I ain't." So father
said, "You'd better do it yourself, Eliza." And she said,
"I will this very day."

So after breakfast Aunt Eliza asked me to show her
where the scuttle was. We always kept it open for fresh
air, except when it rained, and she crawled up through it
and got on the roof. Just then mother called me, and said
it was going to rain, and I must close the scuttle. I began
to tell her that Aunt Eliza was on the roof, but she wouldn't
listen, and said, "Do as I tell you this instant without any
words why can't you obey promptly?" So I obeyed as
prompt as I could, and shut the scuttle and fastened it, and
then went down-stairs, and looked out to see the shower
come up.

It was a tremendous shower, and it struck us in about
ten minutes; and didn't it pour! The wind blew, and it
lightened and thundered every minute, and the street looked
just like a river. I got tired of looking at it after a while,
and sat down to read, and in about an hour, when it was
beginning to rain a little easier, mother came where I was,
and said, "I wonder where sister Eliza is do you know,
Jimmy?" And I said I supposed she was on the roof, for

I left her there when I fastened the scuttle just before it began to rain.

Nothing was done to me until after they had got two men to bring Aunt Eliza down and wring the water out of her, and the doctor had come, and she had been put to bed, and the house was quiet again. By that time father had come home, and when he heard what had happened— But, there! it is over now, and let us say no more about it. Aunt Eliza is as well as ever, but nobody has said a word to me about prompt obedience since the thunder-shower.

OUR ICE-CREAM.

AFTER that trouble with Aunt Eliza—the time she stayed up on the roof and was rained on—I had no misfortunes for nearly a week. Aunt Eliza went home as soon as she was well dried, and father said that he was glad she was gone, for she talked so much all the time that he couldn't hear himself think, though I don't believe he ever did hear himself think. I tried it once. I sat down where it was real still, and thought just as regular and steady as I could : but I couldn't hear the least sound. I suppose our brains are so well oiled that they don't creak at all when we use them. However, Mr. Travers told me of a boy he knew when he was a boy. His name was Ananias G. Smith, and he would run round all day without any hat on, and his hair cut very short, and the sun kept beating on his head all day, and gradually his brains dried so that whenever he tried to think, they would rattle and creak like a wheelbar-row-wheel when it hasn't any grease on it. Of course his parents felt dreadfully, for he couldn't go to school without disturbing everybody as soon as he began to think about his lessons, and he couldn't stay home and think without keeping the baby awake.

As I was saying, there was pretty nearly a whole week that I kept out of trouble; but it didn't last. Boys are born to fly upward like the sparks that trouble, and yesterday I was "up to mischief again," as Sue said, though I never had the least idea of doing any mischief. How should an innocent boy, who might easily have been an orphan had things happened in that way, know all about cooking and chemistry and such, I should like to know.

It was really Sue's fault. Nothing would do but she must give a party, and of course she must have ice-cream. Now the ice-cream that our cake-shop man makes isn't good enough for her, so she got father to buy an ice-cream freezer, and said she would make the ice-cream herself. I was to help her, and she sent me to the store to order some salt. I asked her what she wanted of salt, and she said that you couldn't freeze ice-cream without plenty of salt, and that it was almost as necessary as ice.

I went to the store and ordered the salt, and then had a game or two of ball with the boys, and didn't get home till late in the afternoon. There was Sue freezing the ice-cream, and suffering dreadfully, so she said. She had to go and dress right away, and told me to keep turning the ice-cream freezer till it froze and don't run off and leave me to

SUE'S ICE-CREAM PARTY.

do everything again you good-for-nothing boy I wonder how you can do it.

I turned that freezer for ever so long, but nothing would freeze: so I made up my mind that it wanted more salt. I didn't want to disturb anybody, so I quietly went into the kitchen and got the salt-cellar, and emptied it into the ice-cream. It began to freeze right away; but I tasted it, and it was awfully salt, so I got the jug of golden sirup and poured about a pint into the ice-cream, and when it was done it was a beautiful straw-color.

But there was an awful scene when the party tried to eat that ice-cream. Sue handed it round, and said to everybody, "This is my ice-cream, and you must be sure to like it." The first one she gave it to was Dr. Porter. He is dreadfully fond of ice-cream, and he smiled such a big smile, and said he was sure it was delightful, and took a whole spoonful. Then he jumped up as if something had bit him, and went out of the door in two jumps, and we didn't see him again. Then three more men tasted their ice-cream, and jumped up, and ran after the doctor, and two girls said, "Oh my!" and held their handkerchiefs over their faces, and turned just as pale. And then everybody else put their ice-cream down on the table, and said thank you they guessed they wouldn't take any. The party was regularly spoiled, and when I tasted the ice-cream I didn't wonder.   It was worse than the best kind of strong medicine.

Sue was in a dreadful state of mind, and when the party had gone home—all but one man, who lay under the apple-tree all night and groaned like he was dying, only we thought it was cats—she made me tell her all about the salt and the golden sirup.   She wouldn't believe that I had tried to do my best, and didn't mean any harm.   Father took her part, and said I ought to eat some of the ice-cream, since I made it; but I said I'd rather go up-stairs with him.   So I went.

Some of these days people will begin to understand that they are just wasting and throwing away a boy who always tries to do his best, and perhaps they'll be **sorry** when it is too late.

MY PIG.

I DON'T say that I didn't do wrong, but what I do say is that I meant to do right. But that don't make any difference. It never does. I try to do my very best, and then something happens, and I am blamed for it. When I think what a disappointing world this is, full of bamboo-canes and all sorts of switches, I feel ready to leave it.

It was Sue's fault in the beginning; that is, if it hadn't been for her it wouldn't have happened. One Sunday she and I were sitting in the front parlor, and she was looking out of the window and watching for Mr. Travers; only she said she wasn't, and that she was just looking to see if it was going to rain, and solemnizing her thoughts. I had just asked her how old she was, and couldn't Mr. Travers have been her father if he had married mother, when she said, "Dear me how tiresome that boy is do take a book and read for gracious sake." I said, "What book?" So she gets up and gives me the *Observer*, and says, "There's a beautiful story about a good boy and a pig do read it and keep still if you know how and I hope it will do you some good."

Well, I read the story. It told all about a good boy whose name was James, and his father was poor, and so he kept a pig that cost him twenty-five cents, and when it grew up he sold it for thirty dollars, and he brought the money to his father and said, " Here father! take this O how happy I am to help you when you're old and not good for much," and his father burst into tears, but I don't know what for. I wouldn't burst into tears much if anybody gave me thirty dollars; and said, " Bless you my noble boy you and your sweet pig have saved me from a watery grave," or something like that.

It was a real good story, and it made me feel like being likewise. So I resolved that I would get a little new pig for twenty-five cents, and keep it till it grew up, and then surprise father with twenty-nine dollars, and keep one for myself as a reward for my good conduct. Only I made up my mind not to let anybody know about it till after the pig should be grown up, and then how the family would be delighted with my " thoughtful and generous act!" for that's what the paper said James's act was.

The next day I went to Farmer Smith, and got him to give me a little pig for nothing, only I agreed to help him weed his garden all summer. It was a beautiful pig, about as big as our baby, only it was a deal prettier, and its tail was elegant. I wrapped it up in an old shawl, and watched my chance and got it up into my room, which is on the third story. Then I took my trunk and emptied it, and bored some holes in it for air, and put the pig in it.

I had the best fun that ever was, all that day and the next day, taking care of that dear little pig. I gave him one of my coats for a bed, and fed him on milk, and took him out of the trunk every little while for exercise. Nobody goes into my room very often, except the girl to make the bed, and when she came I shut up the trunk, and she never suspected anything. I got a whole coal-scuttleful of the very best mud, and put it in the corner of the room for him to play in, and when I heard Bridget coming, I meant to throw the bedquilt over it, so she wouldn't suspect anything.

After I had him two days I heard mother say, "Seems to me I hear very queer noises every now and then upstairs." I knew what the matter was, but I never said anything, and I felt so happy when I thought what a good boy I was to raise a pig for my dear father.

Bridget went up to my room about eight o'clock one evening, just before I was going to bed, to take up my clean clothes. We were all sitting in the dining-room, when we heard her holler as if she was being murdered.

We all ran out to see what was the matter, and were half-way up the stairs when the pig came down and upset the whole family, and piled them up on the top of himself at the foot of the stairs, and before we got up Bridget came down and fell over us, and said she had just opened the young masther's thrunk and out jumps the ould Satan himself and she must see the priest or she would be a dead woman.

You wouldn't believe that, though I told them that I was raising the pig to sell it and give the money to father, they all said that they had never heard of such an abandoned and peremptory boy, and father said, " Come up-stairs with me and I'll see if I can't teach you that this house isn't a pig-pen." I don't know what became of the pig, for he broke the parlor window and ran away, and nobody ever heard of him again.

I'd like to see that boy James. I don't care how big he is. I'd show him that he can't go on setting good examples to innocent boys without suffering as he deserves to suffer.

GOING TO BE A PIRATE.

I don't know if you are acquainted with Tom McGinnis. Everybody knows his father, for he's been in Congress, though he is a poor man, and sells hay and potatoes, and I heard father say that Mr. McGinnis is the most remarkable man in the country. Well, Tom is Mr. McGinnis's boy, and he's about my age, and thinks he's tremendously smart; and I used to think so too, but now I don't think quite so much of him. He and I went away to be pirates the other day, and I found out that he will never do for a pirate.

You see, we had both got into difficulties. It wasn't my fault, I am sure, but it's such a painful subject that I won't describe it. I will merely say that after it was all over, I went to see Tom to tell him that it was no use to put shingles under your coat, for how is that going to do your legs any good, and I tried it because Tom advised me to. I found that he had just had a painful scene with his father on account of apples; and I must say it served him right, for he had no business to touch them without permission. So I said, " Look here, Tom, what's the use of our staying at home and being laid onto with switches and our best actions misunderstood and our noblest and holiest emotions held up to ridicule?" That's what I heard a young man say to Sue one day, but it was so beautiful that I said it to Tom myself.

" Oh, go 'way," said Tom.

" That's what I say," said I. " Let's go away and be pirates. There's a brook that runs through Deacon Sammis's woods, and it stands to reason that it must run into the Spanish Main, where all the pirates are. Let's run away, and chop down a tree, and make a canoe, and sail down the brook till we get to the Spanish Main, and then we can capture a schooner, and be regular pirates."

" Hurrah !" says Tom. " We'll do it. Let's run away to-night. I'll take father's hatchet, and the carving-knife, and some provisions, and meet you back of our barn at ten o'clock."

" I'll be there," said I. " Only, if we're going to be pirates, let's be strictly honest. Don't take anything belonging to your father. I've got a hatchet, and a silver knife with my name on it, and I'll save my supper and take it with me."

So that night I watched my chance, and dropped my supper into my handkerchief, and stuffed it into my pocket. When ten o'clock came, I tied up my clothes in a bundle, and took my hatchet and the silver knife and some matches, and slipped out the back door, and met Tom.   He had nothing with him but his supper and a backgammon board and a bag of marbles. We went straight for the woods, and after we'd selected a big tree to cut down, we ate our supper. Just then the moon went under a cloud, and it grew awfully dark. We couldn't see very well how to chop the tree, and after Tom had cut his fingers, we put off cutting down the tree till morning, and resolved to build a fire. We got a lot of fire-wood, but I dropped the matches, and when we found them again they were so damp that they wouldn't light.

All at once the wind began to blow, and made a dreadful moaning in the woods. Tom said it was bears, and that though he wanted to be a pirate, he hadn't calculated on having any bears. Then he said it was cold, and so it was, but I told him that it would be warm enough when we got to the Spanish Main, and that pirates ought not to mind a little cold.

Pretty soon it began to rain, and then Tom began to cry. It just poured down, and the way our teeth chattered was terrible. By-and-by Tom jumped up, and said he wasn't going to be eaten up by bears and get an awful cold, and he started on a run for home. Of course I wasn't going to be a pirate all alone, for there wouldn't be any fun in that,

8

so I started after him. He must have been dreadfully frightened, for he ran as fast as he could, and as I was in a hurry, I tried to catch up with him. If he hadn't tripped over a root, and I hadn't tripped over him, I don't believe I could have caught him. When I fell on him, you ought to have heard him yell. He thought I was a bear, but any sensible pirate would have known I wasn't.

Tom left me at his front gate, and said he had made up his mind he wouldn't be a pirate, and that it would be a great deal more fun to be a plumber and melt lead. I went home, and as the house was locked up, I had to ring the front-door bell. Father came to the door himself, and when he saw me, he said, "Jimmy, what in the world does this mean?" So I told him that Tom and me had started for the Spanish Main to be pirates, but Tom had changed his mind, and that I thought I'd change mine too.

Father had me put to bed, and hot bottles and things put in the bed with me, and before I went to sleep, he came and said, "Good-night, Jimmy. We'll try and have more fun at home, so that there won't be any necessity of your being a pirate." And I said, "Dear father. I'd a good deal rather stay with you, and I'll never be a pirate without your permission."

This is why I say that Tom McGinnis will never make a good pirate. He's too much afraid of getting wet.

RATS AND MICE.

It's queer that girls are so dreadfully afraid of rats and mice. Men are never afraid of them, and I shouldn't mind if there were mornamillion mice in my bedroom every night.

Mr. Travers told Sue and me a terrible story one day about a woman that was walking through a lonely field, when she suddenly saw a field-mouse right in front of her. She was a brave woman; so after she had said, "Oh my! save me, somebody!" she determined to save herself if she could, for there was nobody within miles of her. There was a tree not very far off, and she had just time to climb up the tree and seat herself in the branches, when the mouse reached its foot. There that animal stayed for six days and nights, squeaking in a way that made the woman's blood run cold, and waiting for her to come down. On the seventh day, when she was nearly exhausted, a man with a gun came along, and shot the mouse, and saved her life. I don't believe this story, and I told Mr. Travers so; for a woman couldn't climb a tree, and even if she could, what would hinder the mouse from climbing after her?

Sue has a new young man, who comes every Monday and Wednesday night. One day he said, "Jimmy, if you'll get me a lock of your sister's hair, I'll give you a nice dog." I told him he was awfully kind, but I didn't think it would be honest for me to take Sue's best hair, but that I'd try to get him some of her every-day hair. And he said, "What on earth do you mean, Jimmy?" And I said that Sue had got some new back hair a little while ago, for I was with her when she bought it, and I knew she wouldn't like me to take any of that. So he said it was no matter, and he'd give me the dog anyway.

I told Sue afterwards all about it, just to show her how honest I was, and instead of telling me I was a good boy, she said, "Oh you little torment g'way and never let me see you again," and threw herself down on the sofa and howled dreadfully, and mother came and said, "Jimmy, if you want to kill your dear sister, you can just keep on doing as you do." Such is the gratitude of grown-up folks.

Mr. Withers—that's the new young man—brought the dog, as he said he would. He's a beautiful Scotch terrier, and he said he would kill rats like anything, and was two years old, and had had the distemper; that is, Mr. Withers

SUE HAD OPENED THE BOX.

said the dog would kill rats, and of course Mr. Withers himself never had the distemper.

Of course I wanted to see the dog kill rats, so I took him to a rat-hole in the kitchen, but he barked at it so loud that no rat would think of coming out. If you want to catch rats, you mustn't begin by barking and scratching at rat-holes, but you must sit down and kind of wink with one eye and lay for them, just as cats do. I told Mr. Withers that the dog couldn't catch any rats, and he said he would bring me some in a box, and I could let them out, and the dog would kill every single one of them.

The next evening Sue sent me down to the milliner's to bring her new bonnet home, and don't you be long about it either you idle worthless boy. Well, I went to the milliner's shop, but the bonnet wasn't done yet; and as I passed Mr. Withers's office, he said, "Come here, Jimmy; I've got those rats for you." He gave me a wooden box like a tea-chest, and told me there were a dozen rats in it, and I'd better have the dog kill them at once, or else they'd gnaw out before morning.

When I got home, Sue met me at the door, and said, "Give me that bandbox this instant you've been mornanour about it." I tried to tell her that it wasn't her box; but she wouldn't listen, and just snatched it and went into the parlor, where there were three other young ladies who had come to see her, and slammed the door; but the dog slipped in with her.

In about a minute I heard the most awful yells that anybody ever heard. It sounded as if all the furniture in the parlor was being smashed into kindling wood, and the dog kept barking like mad. The next minute a girl came flying out of the front window, and another girl jumped right on her before she had time to get out of the way, and they never stopped crying, " Help murder let me out oh my!"

I knew, of course, that Sue had opened the box and let the rats out, and though I wanted ever so much to know if the dog had killed them all, I thought she would like it better if I went back to the milliner's and waited a few hours for the bonnet.

I brought it home about nine o'clock; but Sue had gone to bed, and the servant had just swept up the parlor, and piled the pieces of furniture on the piazza. Father won't be home till next week, and perhaps by that time Sue will get over it. I wish I did know if the dog killed all those rats, and how long it took him.

HUNTING THE RHINOCEROS.

WE ought always to be useful, and do good to everybody. I used to think that we ought always to improve
our minds, and I think so some now, though I have got
into dreadful difficulties all through improving my mind.
But I am not going to be discouraged. I tried to be useful
the other day, and do good to the heathen in distant lands,
and you wouldn't believe what trouble it made. There are
some people who would never do good again if they had
got into the trouble that I got into; but the proverb says
that if at first you don't succeed, cry, cry again; and there
was lots of crying, I can tell you, over our rhinoceros, that
we thought was going to do so much good.

It all happened because Aunt Eliza was staying at our
house. She had a Sunday-school one afternoon, and Tom
McGinnis and I were the scholars, and she told us about a
boy that got up a panorama about the *Pilgrim's Progress*
all by himself, and let people see it for ten cents apiece,
and made ten dollars, and sent it to the missionaries, and
they took it and educated mornahundred little heathens

with it, and how nice it would be if you dear boys would go and do likewise and now we'll sing " Hold the Fort."

Well, Tom and I thought about it, and we said we'd get up a menagerie, and we'd take turns playing animals, and we'd let folks see it for ten cents apiece, and make a lot of money, and do ever so much good.

We got a book full of pictures of animals, and we made skins out of cloth to go all over us, so that we'd look just like animals when we had them on. We had a lion's and a tiger's and a bear's and a rhinoceros's skin, besides a whole lot of others. As fast as we got the skins made, we hung them up in a corner of the barn where nobody would see them. The way we made them was to show the pictures to mother and to Aunt Eliza, and they did the cutting out and the sewing, and Sue she painted the stripes on the tiger, and the fancy touches on the other animals.

Our rhinoceros was the best animal we had. The rhinoceros is a lovely animal when he's alive. He is almost as big as an elephant, and he has a skin that is so thick that you can't shoot a bullet through it unless you hit it in a place that is a little softer than the other places. He has a horn on the end of his nose, and he can toss a tiger with it till the tiger feels sick, and says he won't play any more. The rhinoceros lives in Africa, and he would toss 'most all the natives if it wasn't that they fasten an India-rubber ball

THEN HE FELL INTO THE HOT-BED, AND BROKE ALL THE GLASS.

on the end of his horn, so that when he tries to toss any-body, the horn doesn't hurt, and after a while the rhinoce-ros gets discouraged, and says, "Oh, well, what's the good anyhow?" and goes away into the forest. At least this is what Mr. Travers says, but I don't believe it; for the rhi-noceros wouldn't stand still and let the natives put an India-rubber ball on his horn, and they wouldn't want to waste India-rubber balls that way when they could play lawn-tennis with them.

Last Saturday afternoon we had our first grand consol-idated exhibition of the greatest menagerie on earth. We had two rows of chairs in the back yard, and all our folks and all Tom's folks came, and we took in a dollar and sixty cents at the door, which was the back gate.

I was a bear, first of all, and growled so natural that everybody said it was really frightful. Then it was Tom's turn to be an animal, and he was to be the raging rhinoce-ros of Central Africa. I helped dress him in the barn, and when he was dressed he looked beautiful.

The rhinoceros's skin went all over him, and was tied together so that he couldn't get out of it without help. His horn was made of wood painted white, and his eyes were two agates. Of course he couldn't see through them, but they looked natural, and as I was to lead him, he didn't need to see.

I had just got him outside the barn, and had begun to say, " Ladies and gentlemen, this is the raging rhinoceros," when he gave the most awful yell you ever heard, and got up on his hind-legs, and began to rush around as if he was crazy. He rushed against Aunt Eliza, and upset her all over the McGinnis girls, and then he banged up against the water-barrel, and upset that, and then he fell into the hot-bed, and broke all the glass. You never saw such an awful sight. The rhinoceros kept yelling all the time, only nobody could understand what he said, and pulling at his head with his fore-paws, and jumping up and down, and smashing everything in his way, and I went after him just as if I was a Central African hunting a rhinoceros.

I was almost frightened, and as for the folks, they ran into the house, all except Aunt Eliza, who had to be carried in. I kept as close behind the rhinoceros as I could, begging him to be quiet, and tell me what was the matter. After a while he lay down on the ground, and I cut the strings of his skin, so that he could get his head out and talk.

He said he was 'most dead. The wasps had built a nest in one of his hind-legs as it was hanging in the barn, and they had stung him until they got tired. He said he'd never have anything more to do with the menagerie, and went home with his mother, and my mother said I must give him all the money, because he had suffered so much.

But, as I said, I won't be discouraged, and will try to do good, and be useful to others the next time I see a fair chance.

DOWN CELLAR.

We have had a dreadful time at our house, and I have done very wrong. Oh, I always admit it when I've done wrong. There's nothing meaner than to pretend that you haven't done wrong when everybody knows you have. I didn't mean anything by it, though, and Sue ought to have stood by me, when I did it all on her account, and just because I pitied her, if she was my own sister, and it was more her fault, I really think, than it was mine.

Mr. Withers is Sue's new young man, as I have told you already. He comes to see her every Monday, Wednesday, and Friday evening, and Mr. Travers comes all the other evenings, and Mr. Martin is liable to come any time, and generally does—that is, if he doesn't have the rheumatism. Though he hasn't but one real leg, he has twice as much rheumatism as father, with all his legs, and there is something very queer about it; and if I was he, I'd get a leg of something better than cork, and perhaps he'd have less pain in it.

It all happened last Tuesday night. Just as it was get-

ting dark, and Sue was expecting Mr. Travers every minute, who should come in but Mr. Martin! Now Mr. Martin
is such an old acquaintance, and father thinks so much of
him, that Sue had to ask him in, though she didn't want
him to meet Mr. Travers. So when she heard somebody
open the front gate, she said, "Oh, Mr. Martin I'm so
thirsty and the servant has gone out, and you know just
where the milk is for you went down cellar to get some the
last time you were here do you think you would mind getting some for me?" Mr. Martin had often gone down
cellar to help himself to milk, and I don't see what makes
him so fond of it, so he said, "Certainly with great pleasure," and started down the cellar stairs.

It wasn't Mr. Travers, but Mr. Withers, who had come
on the wrong night. He had not much more than got into
the parlor when Sue came rushing out to me, for I was
swinging in the hammock on the front piazza, and said,
"My goodness gracious Jimmy what shall I do here's Mr.
Withers and Mr. Travers will be here in a few minutes and
there's Mr. Martin down cellar and I feel as if I should fly
what shall I do?"

I was real sorry for her, and thought I'd help her, for
girls are not like us. They never know what to do when
they are in a scrape, and they are full of absence of mind
when they ought to have lots of presence of mind. So

9

I said : " I'll fix it for you, Sue. Just leave it all to me
You stay here and meet Mr. Travers, who is just coming
around the corner, and I'll manage Mr. Withers." Sue said,
" You darling little fellow there don't muss my hair ;" and
I went in, and said to Mr. Withers, in an awfully mysteri-
ous way, " Mr. Withers, I hear a noise in the cellar. Don't
tell Sue, for she's dreadfully nervous. Won't you go down
and see what it is?" Of course I knew it was Mr. Martin
who was making the noise, though I didn't say so.

" Oh, it's nothing but rats, Jimmy," said he, " or else the
cat, or maybe it's the cook."

" No, it isn't," said I. " If I was you, I'd go and see
into it. Sue thinks you're awfully brave."

Well, after a little more talk, Mr. Withers said he'd go,
and I showed him the cellar-door, and got him started
down-stairs, and then I locked the door, and went back to
the hammock, and Sue and Mr. Travers they sat in the
front parlor.

Pretty soon I heard a heavy crash down cellar, as if
something heavy had dropped, and then there was such a
yelling and howling, just as if the cellar was full of mur-
derers. Mr. Travers jumped up, and was starting for the
cellar, when Sue fainted away, and hung tight to him, and
wouldn't let him go.

I stayed in the hammock, and wouldn't have left it if

THEY THOUGHT THEY WERE BOTH BURGLARS.

father hadn't come down-stairs, but when I saw him going down cellar, I went after him to see what could possibly be the matter.

Father had a candle in one hand and a big club in another. You ought to have been there to see Mr. Martin and Mr. Withers. One of them had run against the other in the dark, and they thought they were both burglars. So they got hold of each other, and fell over the milk-pans and upset the soap-barrel, and then rolled round the cellar floor, holding on to each other, and yelling help murder thieves, and when we found them, they were both in the ash-bin, and the ashes were choking them.

Father would have pounded them with the club if I hadn't told him who they were. He was awfully astonished, and though he wouldn't say anything to hurt Mr. Martin's feelings, he didn't seem to care much for mine or Mr. Withers's, and when Mr. Travers finally came down, father told him that he was a nice young man, and that the whole house might have been murdered by burglars while he was enjoying himself in the front parlor.

Mr. Martin went home after he got a little of the milk and soap and ashes and things off of him, but he was too angry to speak. Mr. Withers said he would never enter the house again, and Mr. Travers didn't even wait to speak to Sue, he was in such a rage with Mr. Withers. After they were all gone, Sue told father that it was all my fault, and father said he would attend to my case in the morning: only, when the morning came, he told me not to do it again, and that was all.

I admit that I did do wrong, but I didn't mean it, and my only desire was to help my dear sister. You won't catch me helping her again very soon.

OUR BABY AGAIN.

AFTER this, don't say anything more to me about babies. There's nothing more spiteful and militious than a baby. Our baby got me into an awful scrape once—the time I blacked it. But I don't blame it so much that time, because, after all, it was partly my fault; but now it has gone and done one of the meanest things a baby ever did, and came very near ruining me.

It has been a long time since mother and Sue said they would never trust me to take care of the baby again, but the other day they wanted awfully to go to a funeral. It was a funeral of one of their best friends, and there was to be lots of flowers, and they expected to see lots of people, and they said they would try me once more. They were going to be gone about two hours, and I was to take care of the baby till they came home again. Of course I said I would do my best, and so I did; only when a boy does try to do his best, he is sure to get himself into trouble. How many a time and oft have I found this to be true! Ah! this is indeed a hard and hollow world. The last thing Sue said when she went out of the door was, "Now be a good boy if you play any of your tricks I'll let you know." I wish Mr. Travers would marry her, and take her to China. I don't believe in sisters, anyway.

They hadn't been gone ten minutes when the baby woke up and cried, and I knew it did it on purpose. Now I had once read in an old magazine that if you put molasses on a baby's fingers, and give it a feather to play with, it will try to pick that feather off, and amuse itself, and keep quiet for ever so long. I resolved to try it; so I went straight down-stairs and brought up the big molasses jug out of the cellar. Then I made a little hole in one of mother's pillows, and pulled out a good handful of feathers. The baby stopped crying as soon as it saw what I was at, and so led me on, just on purpose to get me into trouble.

Well, I put a little molasses on the baby's hands, and put the feathers in its lap, and told it to be good and play real pretty. The baby began to play with the feathers, just as the magazine said it would, so I thought I would let it enjoy itself while I went up to my room to read a little while.

That baby never made a sound for ever so long, and I was thinking how pleased mother and Sue would be to find out a new plan for keeping it quiet. I just let it enjoy itself till about ten minutes before the time when

they were to get back from the funeral, and then I went
down to mother's room to look after the "little innocent,"
as Sue calls it. Much innocence there is about that baby!

I never saw such a awful spectacle. The baby had got
hold of the molasses jug, which held mornagallon, and had
upset it and rolled all over in it. The feathers had stuck
to it so close that you couldn't hardly see its face, and its
head looked just like a chicken's head. You wouldn't believe how that molasses had spread over the carpet. It
seemed as if about half the room was covered with it.
And there sat that wretched "little innocent" laughing
to think how I'd catch it when the folks came home.

Now wasn't it my duty to wash that baby, and get the
feathers and molasses off it? Any sensible person would
say that it was. I tried to wash it in the wash-basin, but
the feathers kept sticking on again as fast as I got them
off. So I took it to the bath-tub and turned the water on,
and held the baby right under the stream. The feathers
were gradually getting rinsed away, and the molasses was
coming off beautifully, when something happened.

The water made a good deal of noise, and I was standing with my back to the bath-room door, so that I did not
hear anybody come in. The first thing I knew Sue snatched
the baby away, and gave me such a box over the ear.
Then she screamed out, "Ma! come here this wicked boy

is drowning the baby O you little wretch won't you catch it for this." Mother came running up-stairs, and they carried the baby into mother's room to dry it.

You should have heard what they said when Sue slipped and sat down in the middle of the molasses, and cried out that her best dress was ruined, and mother saw what a state the carpet was in! I wouldn't repeat their language for worlds. It was personal, that's what it was, and I've been told fifty times never to make personal remarks. I should not have condescended to notice it if mother hadn't begun to cry; and of course I went and said I was awfully sorry, and that I meant it all for the best, and wouldn't have hurt the baby for anything, and begged her to forgive me and not cry any more.

When father came home they told him all about it. I knew very well they would, and I just lined myself with shingles so as to be good and ready. But he only said, "My son, I have decided to try milder measures with you. I think you are punished enough when you reflect that you have made your mother cry."

That was all, and I tell you I'd rather a hundred times have had him say, "My son, come up-stairs with me." And now if you don't admit that nothing could be meaner than the way that baby acted, I shall really be surprised and shocked.

STUDYING WASPS.

We had a lecture at our place the other day, because our people wanted to get even with the people of the next town, who had had a returned missionary with a whole lot of idols the week before. The lecture was all about wasps and beetles and such, and the lecturer had a magic lantern and a microscope, and everything that was adapted to improve and vitrify the infant mind, as our minister said when he introduced him. I believe the lecturer was a wicked, bad man, who came to our place on purpose to get me into trouble. Else why did he urge the boys to study wasps, and tell us how to collect wasps' nests without getting stung? The grown-up people thought it was all right, however, and Mr. Travers said to me, "Listen to what the gentleman says, Jimmy, and improve your mind with wasps."

Well, I thought I would do as I was told, especially as I knew of a tremendous big wasps' nest under the eaves of our barn. I got a ladder and a lantern the very night after the lecture, and prepared to study wasps. The lecturer said that the way to do was to wait till the wasps go to bed, and then to creep up to their nest with a piece of thin paper all covered with wet mucilage, and to clap it right over the door of the nest. Of course the wasps can't get out when they wake up in the morning, and you can take the nest and hang it up in your room; and after two or three days, when you open the nest and let the wasps out, and feed them with powdered sugar, they'll be so tame and grateful that they'll never think of stinging you, and you can study them all day long, and learn lots of useful lessons. Now is it probable that any real good man would put a boy up to any such nonsense as this? It's my belief that the lecturer was hired by somebody to come and entice all our boys to get themselves stung.

As I was saying, I got a ladder and a lantern, and a piece of paper covered with mucilage, and after dark I climbed up to the wasps' nest, and stopped up the door, and then brought the nest down in my hand. I was going to carry it up to my room, but just then mother called me; so I put the nest under the seat of our carriage, and went into the house, where I was put to bed for having taken the lantern out to the barn; and the next morning I forgot all about the nest.

I forgot it because I was invited to go on a picnic with Mr. Travers and my sister Sue and a whole lot of people, and any fellow would have forgot it if he had been in my place. Mr. Travers borrowed father's carriage, and he and Sue were to sit on the back seat, and Mr. Travers's aunt, who is pretty old and cross, was to sit on the front seat with Dr. Jones, the new minister, and I was to sit with the driver. We all started about nine o'clock, and a big basket of provisions was crowded into the carriage between everybody's feet.

We hadn't gone mornamile when Mr. Travers cries out: "My good gracious! Sue, I've run an awful pin into my leg. Why can't you girls be more careful about pins?" Sue replied that she hadn't any pins where they could run into anybody, and was going to say something more, when she screamed as if she was killed, and began to jump up and down and shake herself. Just then Dr. Jones jumped about two feet straight into the air, and said, "Oh my!" and Miss Travers took to screaming, "Fire! murder! help!" and slapping herself in a way that was quite awful. I began to think they were all going crazy, when all of a sudden I remembered the wasps' nest.

Somehow the wasps had got out of the nest, and were exploring all over the carriage. The driver stopped the horses to see what was the matter, and turned pale with fright when he saw Dr. Jones catch the basket of provisions and throw it out of the carriage, and then jump straight into it. Then Mr. Travers and his aunt and Sue all came flying out together, and were all mixed up with Dr. Jones and the provisions on the side of the road. They didn't stop long, however, for the wasps were looking for them; so they got up and rushed for the river, and went into it as if they were going to drown themselves — only it wasn't more than two feet deep.

George — he's the driver — was beginning to ask, " Is thishyer some swimmin' match that's goin' on?" when a wasp hit him on the neck, and another hit me on the cheek. We left that carriage in a hurry, and I never stopped till I got to my room and rolled myself up in the bedclothes. All the wasps followed me, so that Mr. Travers and Sue and the rest of them were left in peace, and might have gone to the picnic, only they felt as if they must come home for arnica, and, besides, the horses had run away, though they were caught afterwards, and didn't break anything.

This was all because that lecturer advised me to study wasps. I followed his directions, and it wasn't my fault that the wasps began to study Mr. Travers and his aunt, and Sue and Dr. Jones, and me and George. But father, when he was told about it, said that my " conduct was such," and the only thing that saved me was that my legs were stung all over, and father said he didn't have the heart to do any more to them with a switch.

A TERRIBLE MISTAKE.

I HAVE been in the back bedroom up-stairs all the afternoon, and I am expecting father every minute. It was just after one o'clock when he told me to come up-stairs with him, and just then Mr. Thompson came to get him to go down town with him, and father said I'd have to excuse him for a little while and don't you go out of that room till I come back. So I excused him, and he hasn't come back yet; but I've opened one of the pillows and stuffed my clothes full of feathers, and I don't care much how soon he comes back now.

It's an awful feeling to be waiting up-stairs for your father, and to know that you have done wrong, though you really didn't mean to do so much wrong as you have done. I am willing to own that nobody ought to take anybody's clothes when he's in swimming, but anyhow they began it first, and I thought just as much as could be that the clothes were theirs.

The real boys that are to blame are Joe Wilson and Amzi Willetts. A week ago Saturday Tom McGinnis and I went in swimming down at the island. It's a beautiful place. The island is all full of bushes, and on one side the water is deep, where the big boys go in, and on the other it is shallow, where we fellows that can't swim very much where the water is more than two feet deep go in. While Tom and I were swimming, Joe and Amzi came and stole our clothes, and put them in their boat, and carried them clear across the deep part of the river. We saw them do it, and we had an awful time to get the clothes back, and I think it was just as mean.

Tom and I said we'd get even with them, and I know it was wrong, because it was a revengeful feeling, but anyhow we said we'd do it; and I don't think revenge is so very bad when you don't hurt a fellow, and wouldn't hurt him for anything, and just want to play him a trick that is pretty nearly almost quite innocent. But I don't say we did right, and when I've done wrong I'm always ready to say so.

Well, Tom and I watched, and last Saturday we saw Joe and Amzi go down to the island, and go in swimming on the shallow side; so we waded across and sneaked down among the bushes, and after a while we saw two piles of clothes. So we picked them up and ran away with them. The boys saw us, and made a terrible noise; but we sung out that they'd know now how it felt to have your clothes carried off, and we waded back across the river, and carried the clothes up to Amzi's house, and hid them in his barn, and thought that we'd got even with Joe and Amzi, and taught them a lesson which would do them a great deal of good, and would make them good and useful men.

This was in the morning about noon, and when I had my dinner I thought I'd go and see how the boys liked swimming, and offer to bring back their clothes if they'd promise to be good friends. I never was more astonished in my life than I was to find that they were nowhere near the island. I was beginning to be afraid they'd been drowned, when I heard some men calling me, and I found Squire Meredith and Amzi Willetts's father, who is a deacon, hiding among the bushes. They told me that some villains had stolen their clothes while they were in swimming, and they'd give me fifty cents if I'd go up to their houses and get their wives to give me some clothes to bring down to them.

I said I didn't want the fifty cents, but I'd go and try to find some clothes for them. I meant to go straight up to Amzi's barn and to bring the clothes back, but on the way I met Amzi with the clothes in a basket bringing them down to the island, and he said, "Somebody's goin' to be arrested for stealing father's and Squire Meredith's clothes. I saw the fellows that stole 'em, and I'm going to tell." You see, Tom and I had taken the wrong clothes, and

10

Squire Meredith and Deacon Willetts, who had been in swimming on the deep side of the island, had been about two hours trying to play they were Zulus, and didn't need to wear any clothes, only they found it pretty hard work.

Deacon Willetts came straight to our house, and told father that his unhappy son—that's what he called me, and wasn't I unhappy, though—had stolen his clothes and Squire Meredith's; but for the sake of our family he wouldn't say very much about it, only if father thought best to spare the rods and spoil a child, he wouldn't be able to regard him as a man and a brother. So father called me and asked me if I had taken Deacon Willetts's clothes, and when I said yes, and was going to explain how it happened, he said that my conduct was such, and that I was bringing his gray hairs down, only I wouldn't hurt them for fifty million dollars, and I've often heard him say he hadn't a gray hair in his head.

And now I'm waiting up-stairs for the awful moment to arrive. I deserve it, for they say that Squire Meredith and Deacon Willetts are mornhalf eaten up by mosquitoes, and are confined to the house with salt and water, and crying out all the time that they can't stand it. I hope the feathers will work, but if they don't, no matter. I think I shall be a missionary, and do good to the heathen. I think I hear father coming in the front gate now, so I must close.

OUR BULL-FIGHT.

I'm going to stop improving my mind. It gets me into trouble all the time. Grown-up folks can improve their minds without doing any harm, for nobody ever tells them that their conduct is such, and that there isn't the least excuse in the world for them; but just as sure as a boy tries to improve his mind, especially with animals, he gets into dreadful difficulties.

There was a man came to our town to lecture a while ago. He had been a great traveller, and knew all about Rome and Niagara Falls and the North Pole, and such places, and father said, "Now, Jimmy, here's an opportunity for you to learn something and improve your mind go and take your mother and do take an interest in something besides games."

Well, I went to the lecture. The man told all about the Australian savages and their boomerangs. He showed us a boomerang, which is a stick with two legs, and an Australian will throw it at a man, and it will go and hit him, and come back of its own accord. Then he told us about the way the Zulus throw their assegais — that's the right way to spell it—and spear an Englishman that is mornten rods away from them. Then he showed a long string with a heavy lead ball on each end, and said the South Americans would throw it at a wild horse, and it would wind around the horse's legs, and tie itself into a bow-knot, and then the South Americans would catch the horse. But the best of all was the account of a bull-fight which he saw in Spain, with the Queen sitting on a throne, and giving a crown of evergreens to the chief bull-fighter. He said that bull-fighting was awfully cruel, and that he told us about it so that we might be thankful that we are so much better than those dreadful Spanish people, who will watch a bull-fight all day, and think it real fun.

The next day I told Mr. Travers about the boomerang, and he said it was all true. Once there was an Australian savage in a circus, and he got angry, and he threw his boomerang at a man who was in the third story of a hotel. The boomerang went down one street and up another, and into the hotel door, and up-stairs, and knocked the man on the head, and came back the same way right into the Australian savage's hand.

I was so anxious to show father that I had listened to the lecture that I made a boomerang just like the one the lecturer had. When it was done, I went out into the back yard, and slung it at a cat on the roof of our house. It never touched the cat, but it went right through the dining-room window, and gave Mr. Travers an awful blow in the eye, besides hitting Sue on the nose. It stopped right there in the dining-room, and never came back to me at all, and I don't believe a word the lecturer said about it. I don't feel courage to tell what father said about it.

Then I tried to catch Mr. Thompson's dog, that lives next door to us, with two lead balls tied on the ends of a long string. I didn't hit the dog any more than I did the cat, but I didn't do any harm except to Mrs. Thompson's cook, and she ought to be thankful that it was only her arm, for the doctor said that if the balls had hit her on the head they would have broken it, and the consequences might have been serious.

It was a good while before I could find anything to make an assegai out of; but after hunting all over the house, I came across a lovely piece of bamboo about ten feet long, and just as light as a feather. Then I got a big knife-blade that hadn't any handle to it, and that had been lying in father's tool-chest for ever so long, and fastened it on the end of the bamboo. You wouldn't believe how splendidly I could throw that assegai, only the wind would take it, and you couldn't tell when you threw it where it would bring up. I don't see how the Zulus ever manage to hit an Englishman; but Mr. Travers says that the Englishmen are all so made that you can't very well miss them. And then perhaps the Zulus, when they want to hit them, aim at something else. One day I was practising with the assegai at our barn-door, making believe that it was an Englishman, when Mr. Carruthers, the butcher, drove by, and the assegai came down and went through his foot, and pinned it to the wagon. But he didn't see me, and I guess he got it out after a while, though I never saw it again.

But what the lecturer taught us about bull-fights was worse than anything else. Tom McGinnis's father has a terrible bull in the pasture, and Tom and I agreed that we'd have a bull-fight, only, of course, we wouldn't hurt the bull. All we wanted to do was to show our parents how much we had learned about the geography and habits of the Spaniards.

Tom McGinnis's sister Jane, who is twelve years old, and thinks she knows everything, said she'd be the Queen of Spain, and give Tom and me evergreen wreaths. I got an old red curtain out of the dining-room, and divided it with Tom, so that we could wave it in the bull's face. When a bull runs after a bull-fighter, the other bull-fighter just waves his red rag, and the bull goes for him and lets the first bull-fighter escape. The lecturer said that there wasn't any danger so long as one fellow would always wave a red rag when the bull ran after the other fellow.

HE WENT TWENTY FEET RIGHT UP INTO THE AIR.

Pretty nearly all the school came down to the pasture to see our bull-fight. The Queen of Spain sat on the fence, because there wasn't any other throne, and the rest of the fellows and girls stood behind the fence. The bull was pretty savage; but Tom and I had our red rags, and we weren't afraid of him.

As soon as we went into the pasture the bull came for me, with his head down, and bellowing as if he was out of his mind. Tom rushed up and waved his red rag, and the bull stopped running after me, and went after Tom, just as the lecturer said he would.

I know I ought to have waved my red rag, so as to rescue Tom, but I was so interested that I forgot all about it, and the bull caught up with Tom. I should think he went twenty feet right up into the air, and as he came down he hit the Queen of Spain, and knocked her about six feet right against Mr. McGinnis, who had come down to the pasture to stop the fight.

The doctor says they'll all get well, though Tom's legs are all broke, and his sister's shoulder is out of joint, and Mr. McGinnis has got to get a new set of teeth. Father didn't do a thing to me—that is, with anything—but he talked to me till I made up my mind that I'd never try to learn anything from a lecturer again, not even if he lectures about Indians and scalping-knives.

OUR BALLOON.

I've made up my mind that half the trouble boys get into is the fault of the grown-up folks that are always wanting them to improve their minds.

I never improved my mind yet without suffering for it. There was the time I improved it studying wasps, just as the man who lectured about wasps and elephants and other insects told me to. If it hadn't been for that man I never should have thought of studying wasps.

One time our school-teacher told me that I ought to improve my mind by reading history, so I borrowed the history of *Blackbeard the Pirate*, and improved my mind for three or four hours every day. After a while father said, "Bring that book to me, Jimmy, and let's see what you're reading," and when he saw it, instead of praising me, he— But what's the use of remembering our misfortunes? Still, if I was grown up, I wouldn't get boys into difficulty by telling them to do all sorts of things.

There was a Professor came to our house the other day. A Professor is a kind of man who wears spectacles up on the top of his head and takes snuff and doesn't talk English very plain. I believe Professors come from somewhere near Germany, and I wish this one had stayed in his own country. They live mostly on cabbage and such, and Mr. Travers says they are dreadfully fierce, and that when they are not at war with other people, they fight among themselves, and go on in the most dreadful way.

This Professor that came to see father didn't look a bit fierce, but Mr. Travers says that was just his deceitful way, and that if we had had a valuable old bone or a queer kind of shell in the house, the Professor would have got up in the night, and stolen it and killed us all in our beds; but Sue said it was a shame, and that the Professor was a lovely old gentleman, and there wasn't the least harm in his kissing her.

Well, the Professor was talking after dinner to father about balloons, and when he saw I was listening, he pretended to be awfully kind, and told me how to make a fire-balloon, and how he'd often made them and sent them up in the air; and then he told about a man who went up on horseback with his horse tied to a balloon; and father said, "Now listen to the Professor, Jimmy, and improve your mind while you've got a chance."

The next day Tom McGinnis and I made a balloon just as the Professor had told me to. It was made out of tissue-paper, and it had a sponge soaked full of alcohol, and when you set the alcohol on fire the tumefaction of the air would send the balloon mornamile high. We made it out in the barn, and thought we'd try it before we said anything to the folks about it, and then surprise them by showing them what a beautiful balloon we had, and how we'd improved our minds. Just as it was all ready, Sue's cat came into the barn, and I remembered the horse that had been tied to a balloon, and told Tom we'd see if the balloon would take the cat up with it.

So we tied her with a whole lot of things so she would hang under the balloon without being hurt a bit, and then we took the balloon into the yard to try it. After the alcohol had burned a little while the balloon got full of air, and presently it went slowly up. There wasn't a bit of wind, and when it had gone up about twice as high as the house it stood still.

You ought to have seen how that cat howled; but she was nothing compared with Sue when she came out and saw her beloved beast. She screamed to me to bring her that cat this instant you good-for-nothing cruel little wretch won't you catch it when father comes home.

Now I'd like to know how I could reach a cat that was a hundred feet up in the air, but that's all the reasonableness that girls have.

PRESENTLY IT WENT SLOWLY UP.

The balloon didn't stay up very long. It began to come slowly down, and when it struck the ground, the way that cat started on a run for the barn, and tried to get underneath it with the balloon all on fire behind her, was something frightful to see. By the time I could get to her and cut her loose, a lot of hay took fire and began to blaze, and Tom ran for the fire-engine, crying out " Fire!" with all his might.

The firemen happened to be at the engine-house, though they're generally all over town, and nobody can find them when there is a fire. They brought the engine into our yard in about ten minutes, and just as Sue and the cook and I had put the fire out. But that didn't prevent the firemen from working with heroic bravery, as our newspaper afterwards said. They knocked in our dining-room windows with axes, and poured about a thousand hogsheads of water into the room before we could make them understand that the fire was down by the barn, and had been put out before they came.

This was all the Professor's fault, and it has taught me a lesson. The next time anybody wants me to improve my mind I'll tell him he ought to be ashamed of himself.

OUR NEW WALK.

For once I have done right. I always used to think that if I stuck to it, and tried to do what was right, I would hit it some day; but at last I pretty nearly gave up all hope, and was beginning to believe that no matter what I did, some of the grown-up folks would tell me that my conduct was such. But I have done a real useful thing that was just what father wanted, and he has said that he would overlook it this time. Perhaps you think that this was not very encouraging to a boy; but if you had been told to come up-stairs with me my son as often as I have been, just because you had tried to do right, and hadn't exactly managed to suit people, you would be very glad to hear your father say that for once he would overlook it.

Did you ever play you were a ghost? I don't think much of ghosts, and wouldn't be a bit afraid if I was to see one. There was once a ghost that used to frighten people dreadfully by hanging himself to a hook in the wall. He was one of those tall white ghosts, and they are the very worst kind there is. This one used to come into the spare bedroom of the house where he lived before he was dead, and after walking round the room, and making as if he was in dreadfully low spirits, he would take a rope out of his pocket, and hang himself to a clothes-hook just opposite the bed, and the person who was in the bed would faint away with fright, and pull the bedclothes over his head, and lie in the most dreadful agony until morning, when he would get up, and people would say, " Why how dreadful you look your hair is all gray and you are whiternany sheet." One time a man came to stay at the house who wasn't afraid of anything, and he said, " I'll fix that ghost of yours; I'm a terror on wooden wheels when any ghosts are around, I am." So he was put to sleep in the room, and before he went to bed he loosened the hook, so that it would come down very easy, and then he sat up in bed and read till twelve o'clock. Just when the clock struck, the ghost came in and walked up and down as usual, and finally got out his rope and hung himself; but as soon as he kicked away the chair he stood on when he hung himself, down came the hook, and the ghost fell all in a heap on the floor, and sprained his ankle, and got up and limped away, dreadfully ashamed, and nobody ever saw him again.

Father has been having the front garden walk fixed with an askfelt pavement. Askfelt is something like molasses, only four times as sticky when it is new. After a while it

11

grows real hard, only ours hasn't grown very hard yet. I watched the men put it down, and father said, " Be careful and don't step on it until it gets hard or you'll stick fast in it and can't ever get out again. I'd like to see half a dozen meddlesome boys stuck in it and serve them right." As soon as I heard dear father mention what he'd like, I determined that he should have his wish, for there is nothing that is more delightful to a good boy than to please his father.

That afternoon I mentioned to two or three boys that I knew were pretty bad boys that our melons were ripe, and that father was going to pick them in a day or two. The melon patch is at the back of the house, and after dark I dressed myself in one of mother's gowns, and hid in the wood-shed. About eleven o'clock I heard a noise, and looked out, and there were six boys coming in the back gate, and going for the melon patch. I waited till they were just ready to begin, and then I came out and said, in a hollow and protuberant voice, " Beware !"

They dropped the melons, and started to run, but they couldn't get to the back gate without passing close to me, and I knew they wouldn't try that. So they started to run round the house to the front gate, and I ran after them. When they reached the new front walk, they seemed to stop all of a sudden, and two or three of them fell down.

PRYING THE BOYS OUT.

I didn't wait to hear what they had to say, but went quietly back, and got into the house through the kitchen-window, and went up-stairs to my room. I could hear them whispering, and now and then one or two of them would cry a little; but I thought it wouldn't be honorable to listen to them, so I went to sleep.

In the morning there were five boys stuck in the askfelt, and frightened 'most to death. I got up early, and called father, and told him that there seemed to be something the matter with his new walk. When he came out and saw five boys caught in the pavement, and an extra pair of shoes that belonged to another boy who had wriggled out of them and gone away and left them, he was the most astonished man you ever saw. I told him how I had caught the boys stealing melons, and had played I was a ghost and frightened them away, and he said that if I'd help the coachman pry the boys out, he would overlook it. So he sat upon the piazza and overlooked the coachman and me while we pried the boys out, and they came out awfully hard, and the askfelt is full of pieces of trousers and things. I don't believe it will ever be a handsome walk; but whenever father looks at it he will think what a good boy I have been, which will give him more pleasure than a hundred new askfelt walks.

A STEAM CHAIR.

I don't like Mr. Travers as much as I did. Of course I know he's a very nice man, and he's going to be my brother when he marries Sue, and he used to bring me candy sometimes, but he isn't what he used to be.

One time—that was last summer—he was always dreadfully anxious to hear from the Post-office, and whenever he came to see Sue, and he and she and I would be sitting on the front piazza, he would say, "Jimmy, I think there must be a letter for me; I'll give you ten cents if you'll go down to the Post-office;" and then Sue would say, "Don't run, Jimmy; you'll get heart disease if you do;" and I'd walk 'way down to the Post-office, which is pretty near half a mile from our house. But now he doesn't seem to care anything about his letters; and he and Sue sit in the back parlor, and mother says I mustn't go in and disturb them; and I don't get any more ten cents.

I've learned that it won't do to fix your affections on human beings, for even the best of men won't keep on giving you ten cents forever. And it wasn't fair for Mr. Travers to get angry with me the other night, when it was all an accident—at least 'most all of it; and I don't think it's manly for a man to stand by and see a sister shake a fellow that isn't half her size, and especially when he never supposed that anything was going to happen to her even if it did break.

When Aunt Eliza came to our house the last time, she brought a steam chair: that's what she called it, though there wasn't any steam about it. She brought it from Europe with her, and it was the queerest sort of chair, that would all fold up, and had a kind of footstool to it, so that you put your legs out and just lie down in it. Well, one day it got broken. The back of the seat fell down, and shut Aunt Eliza up in the chair so she couldn't get out, and didn't she just howl till somebody came and helped her! She was so angry that she said she never wanted to see that chair again, and you may have it if you want it Jimmy for you are a good boy sometimes when you want to be.

So I took the chair and mended it. The folks laughed at me, and said I couldn't mend it to save my life; but I got some nails and some mucilage, and mended it elegantly. Then mother let me get some varnish, and I varnished the chair, and when it was done it looked so nice that Sue said we'd keep it in the back parlor. Now I'm never allowed to sit in the back parlor, so what good would my chair do me? But Sue said, "Stuff and nonsense that boy's indulged now till he can't rest." So they put my chair in the back parlor, just as if I'd been mending it on purpose for Mr. Travers. I didn't say anything more about it; but after it was in the back parlor I took out one or two screws that I thought were not needed to hold it together, and used them for a boat that I was making.

That night Mr. Travers came as usual, and after he had talked to mother awhile about the weather, and he and father had agreed that it was a shame that other folks hadn't given more money to the Michigan sufferers, and that they weren't quite sure that the sufferers were a worthy object, and that a good deal of harm was done by giving away money to all sorts of people, Sue said,

"Perhaps we had better go into the back parlor; it is cooler there, and we won't disturb father, who wants to think about something."

So she and Mr. Travers went into the back parlor, and shut the door, and talked very loud at first about a whole lot of things, and then quieted down, as they always did.

I was in the front parlor, reading "Robinson Crusoe," and wishing I could go and do likewise—like Crusoe, I mean; for I wouldn't go and sit quietly in a back parlor with a girl, like Mr. Travers, not if you were to pay me for

IT HAD SHUT UP LIKE A JACK-KNIFE.

it. I can't see what some fellows see in Sue. I'm sure if Mr. Martin or Mr. Travers had her pull their hair once the way she pulls mine sometimes, they wouldn't trust themselves alone with her very soon.

All at once we heard a dreadful crash in the back parlor, and Mr. Travers said Good something very loud, and Sue shrieked as if she had a needle run into her. Father and mother and I and the cook and the chambermaid all rushed to see what was the matter.

The chair that I had mended, and that Sue had taken away from me, had broken down while Mr. Travers was sitting in it, and it had shut up like a jack-knife, and caught him so he couldn't get out. It had caught Sue too, who must have run to help him, or she never would have been in that fix, with Mr. Travers holding her by the waist, and her arm wedged in so she couldn't pull it away.

Father managed to get them loose, and then Sue caught me and shook me till I could hear my teeth rattle, and then she ran up-stairs and locked herself up; and Mr. Travers never offered to help me, but only said, "I'll settle with you some day, young man," and then he went home. But father sat down on the sofa and laughed, and said to mother,

"I guess Sue would have done better if she'd have let the boy keep his chair."

ANIMALS.

I should like to be an animal. Not an insect, of course, nor a snake, but a nice kind of animal, like an elephant or a dog with a good master.

Animals are awfully intelligent, but they haven't any souls. There was once an elephant in a circus, and one day a boy said to him, "Want a lump of sugar, old fellow?" The elephant he nodded, and felt real grateful, for elephants are very fond of lump-sugar, which is what they live on in their native forests. But the boy put a cigar instead of a lump of sugar in his mouth.

The sagacious animal, instead of eating up the cigar or trying to smoke it and making himself dreadfully sick, took it and carried it across the circus to a man who kept a candy and cigar stand, and made signs that he'd sell the cigar for twelve lumps of sugar. The man gave the elephant the sugar and took the cigar, and then the intelligent animal sat down on his hind-legs and laughed at the boy who had tried to play a joke on him, until the boy felt that much ashamed that he went right home and went to bed.

In the days when there were fairies—only I don't believe there ever were any fairies, and Mr. Travers says they were rubbish—boys were frequently changed into animals. There was once a boy who did something that made a wicked fairy angry, and she changed him into a cat, and thought she had punished him dreadfully. But the boy after he was a cat used to come and get on her back fence and yowl as if he was ten or twelve cats all night long, and she couldn't get a wink of sleep, and fell into a fever, and had to take lots of castor-oil and dreadful medicines.

So she sent for the boy who was a cat, you understand, and said she'd change him back again. But he said, "Oh no; I'd much rather be a cat, for I'm so fond of singing on the back fence." And the end of it was that she had to give him a tremendous pile of money before he'd consent to be changed back into a boy again.

Boys can play being animals, and it's great fun, only the other boys who don't play they are animals get punished for it, and I say it's unjust, especially as I never meant any harm at all, and was doing my very best to amuse the children.

This is the way it happened. Aunt Sarah came to see us the other day, and brought her three boys with her. I don't think you ever heard of Aunt Sarah, and I wish I never had. She's one of father's sisters, and he thinks a great deal more of her than I would if she was my sister, and I don't think it's much credit to anybody to be a sister anyway. The boys are twins, that is, two of them are, and they are all about three or four years old.

Well, one day just before Christmas, when it was almost as warm out-doors as it is in summer, Aunt Sarah said,

"Jimmy, I want you to take the dear children out and amuse them a few hours. I know you're so fond of your dear little cousins and what a fine manly boy you are!" So I took them out, though I didn't want to waste my time with little children, for we are responsible for wasting time, and ought to use every minute to improve ourselves.

The boys wanted to see the pigs that belong to Mr. Taylor, who lives next door, so I took them through a hole in the fence, and they looked at the pigs, and one of them said,

"Oh my how sweet they are and how I would like to be a little pig and never be washed and have lots of swill!"

So I said, "Why don't you play you are pigs, and crawl round and grunt? It's just as easy, and I'll look at you."

You see, I thought I ought to amuse them, and that this would be a nice way to teach them to amuse themselves.

Well, they got down on all fours and ran round and grunted, until they began to get tired of it, and then wanted to know what else pigs could do, so I told them that pigs generally rolled in the mud, and the more mud a pig could

"WE'VE BEEN PLAYING WE WERE PIGS, MA."

get on himself the happier he would be, and that there was a mud puddle in our back yard that would make a pig cry like a child with delight.

The boys went straight to that mud puddle, and they rolled in the mud until there wasn't an inch of them that wasn't covered with mud so thick that you would have to get a crowbar to pry it off.

Just then Aunt Sarah came to the door and called them, and when she saw them she said, "Good gracious what on earth have you been doing?" and Tommy, that's the oldest boy, said,

"We've been playing we were pigs ma and it's real fun and wasn't Jimmy good to show us how?"

I think they had to boil the boys in hot water before they could get the mud off, and their clothes have all got to be sent to the poor people out West whose things were all lost in the great floods. If you'll believe it, I never got the least bit of thanks for showing the boys how to amuse themselves, but Aunt Sarah said that I'd get something when father came home, and she wasn't mistaken. I'd rather not mention what it was that I got, but I got it mostly on the legs, and I think bamboo canes ought not to be sold to fathers any more than poison.

I was going to tell why I should like to be an animal; but as it is getting late, I must close.

12

A PLEASING EXPERIMENT.

EVERY time I try to improve my mind with science I resolve that I will never do it again, and then I always go and do it. Science is so dreadfully tempting that you can hardly resist it. Mr. Travers says that if anybody once gets into the habit of being a scientific person there is little hope that he will ever reform, and he says he has known good men who became habitual astronomers, and actually took to prophesying weather, all because they yielded to the temptation to look through telescopes, and to make figures on the black-board with chalk.

I was reading a lovely book the other day. It was all about balloons and parachutes. A parachute is a thing that you fall out of a balloon with. It is something like an open umbrella, only nobody ever borrows it. If you hold a parachute over your head and drop out of a balloon, it will hold you up so that you will come down to the ground so gently that you won't be hurt the least bit.

I told Tom McGinnis about it, and we said we would make a parachute, and jump out of the second-story win dow with it. It is easy enough to make one, for all you have to do is to get a big umbrella and open it wide, and hold on to the handle. Last Saturday afternoon Tom came over to my house, and we got ready to try what the book said was "a pleasing scientific experiment."

We didn't have the least doubt that the book told the truth. But Tom didn't want to be the first to jump out of the window—neither did I—and we thought we'd give Sue's kitten a chance to try a parachute, and see how she liked it. Sue had an umbrella that was made of silk, and was just the thing to suit the kitten. I knew Sue wouldn't mind lending the umbrella, and as she was out making calls, and I couldn't ask her permission, I borrowed the umbrella and the kitten, and meant to tell her all about it as soon as she came home. We tied the kitten fast to the handle of the umbrella, so as not to hurt her, and then dropped her out of the window. The wind was blowing tremendously hard, which I supposed was a good thing, for it is the air that holds up a parachute, and of course the more wind there is, the more air there is, and the better the parachute will stay up.

The minute we dropped the cat and the umbrella out of the window, the wind took them and blew them clear over the back fence into Deacon Smedley's pasture before they struck the ground. This was all right enough, but the

parachute didn't stop after it struck the ground.   It started
across the country about as fast as a horse could run, hitting the ground every few minutes, and then bouncing up
into the air and coming down again, and the kitten kept
clawing at everything, and yowling as if she was being
killed. By the time Tom and I could get down-stairs the
umbrella was about a quarter of a mile off. We chased it
till we couldn't run any longer, but we couldn't catch it,
and the last we saw of the umbrella and the cat they
were making splendid time towards the river, and I'm
very much afraid they were both drowned.

Tom and I came home again, and when we got a little
rested we said we would take the big umbrella and try the
pleasing scientific experiment; at least I said that Tom
ought to try it. for we had proved that a little silk umbrella would let a kitten down to the ground without hurting her, and of course a great big umbrella would hold
Tom up all right. I didn't care to try it myself, because
Tom was visiting me, and we ought always to give up our
own pleasures in order to make our visitors happy.

After a while Tom said he would do it, and when every
thing was ready he sat on the window-ledge, with his legs
hanging out, and when the wind blew hard he jumped.

It is my opinion, now that the thing is all over, that the
umbrella wasn't large enough, and that if Tom had struck

HE LIT RIGHT ON THE MAN'S HEAD.

the ground he would have been hurt. He went down awfully fast, but by good-luck the grocer's man was just coming out of the kitchen-door as Tom came down, and he lit right on the man's head. It is wonderful how lucky some people are, for the grocer's man might have been hurt if he hadn't happened to have a bushel basket half full of eggs with him, and as he and Tom both fell into the eggs, neither of them was hurt.

They were just getting out from among the eggs when Sue came in with some of the ribs of her umbrella that somebody had fished out of the river and given to her. There didn't seem to be any kitten left, for Sue didn't know anything about it, but father and Mr. McGinnis came in a few minutes afterwards, and I had to explain the whole thing to them.

This is the last " pleasing scientific experiment" I shall ever try. I don't think science is at all nice, and, besides, I am awfully sorry about the kitten.

TRAPS.

A BOY ought always to stand up for his sister, and protect her from everybody, and do everything to make her happy, for she can only be his sister once, and he would be so awfully sorry if she died and then he remembered that his conduct towards her had sometimes been such.

Mr. Withers doesn't come to our house any more. One night Sue saw him coming up the garden-walk, and father said, "There's the other one coming, Susan; isn't this Travers's evening?" and then Sue said, "I do wish somebody would protect me from him he is that stupid don't I wish I need never lay eyes on him again."

I made up my mind that nobody should bother my sister while she had a brother to protect her. So the next time I saw Mr. Withers I spoke to him kindly and firmly—that's the way grown-up people speak when they say something dreadfully unpleasant—and told him what Sue had said about him, and that he ought not to bother her any more. Mr. Withers didn't thank me and say that he knew I was trying to do him good, which was what he ought to have said, but he looked as if he wanted to hurt somebody, and walked off without saying a word to me, and I don't think he was polite about it.

He has never been at our house since. When I told Sue how I had protected her she was so overcome with gratitude that she couldn't speak, and just motioned me with a book to go out of her room and leave her to feel thankful about it by herself. The book very nearly hit me on the head, but it wouldn't have hurt much if it had.

Mr. Travers was delighted about it, and told me that I had acted like a man, and that he shouldn't forget it. The next day he brought me a beautiful book all about traps. It told how to make mornahundred different kinds of traps that would catch everything, and it was one of the best books I ever saw.

Our next-door neighbor, Mr. Schofield, keeps pigs, only he don't keep them enough, for they run all around. They come into our garden and eat up everything, and father said he would give almost anything to get rid of them.

Now one of the traps that my book told about was just the thing to catch pigs with. It was made out of a young tree and a rope. You bend the tree down and fasten the rope to it so as to make a slippernoose, and when the pig walks into the slippernoose the tree flies up and jerks him into the air.

I thought that I couldn't please father better than to make some traps and catch some pigs; so I got a rope, and got two Irishmen that were fixing the front walk to bend down two trees for me and hold them while I made the traps. This was just before supper, and I expected that the pigs would come early the next morning and get caught.

It was bright moonlight that evening, and Mr. Travers and Sue said the house was so dreadfully hot that they would go and take a walk. They hadn't been out of the house but a few minutes when we heard an awful shriek from Sue, and we all rushed out to see what was the matter.

Mr. Travers had walked into a trap, and was swinging by one leg, with his head about six feet from the ground. Nobody knew him at first except me, for when a person is upside down he doesn't look natural; but I knew what was the matter, and told father that it would take two men to bend down the tree and get Mr. Travers loose. So they told me to run and get Mr. Schofield to come and help, and they got the step-ladder so that Sue could sit on the top of it and hold Mr. Travers's head.

I was so excited that I forgot all about the other trap, and, besides, Sue had said things to me that hurt my feelings, and that prevented me from thinking to tell Mr. Schofield not to get himself caught. He ran ahead of me, because he was so anxious to help, and the first thing I knew there came an awful yell from him, and up he went into the air, and hung there by both legs, which I suppose was easier than the way Mr. Travers hung.

Then everybody went at me in the most dreadful way, except Sue, who was holding Mr. Travers's head. They said the most unkind things to me, and sent me into the house. I heard afterwards that father got Mr. Schofield's boy to climb up and cut Mr. Travers and Mr. Schofield loose, and they fell on the gravel, but it didn't hurt them much, only Mr. Schofield broke some of his teeth, and says he is going to bring a lawsuit against father. Mr. Travers was just as good as he could be. He only laughed the next time he saw me, and he begged them not to punish me, because it was his fault that I ever came to know about that kind of trap.

Mr. Travers is the nicest man that ever lived, except father, and when he marries Sue I shall go and live with him, though I haven't told him yet, for I want to keep it as a pleasant surprise for him.

AN ACCIDENT.

Aunt Eliza never comes to our house without getting me into difficulties. I don't really think she means to do it, but it gets itself done just the same. She was at our house last week, and though I meant to behave in the most exemplifying manner, I happened by accident to do something which she said ought to fill me with remorse for the rest of my days.

Remorse is a dreadful thing to have. Some people have it so bad that they never get over it. There was once a ghost who suffered dreadfully from remorse. He was a tall white ghost, with a large cotton umbrella. He haunted a house where he used to walk up and down, carrying his umbrella and looking awfully solemn. People used to wonder what he wanted of an umbrella, but they never asked him, because they always shrieked and fainted away when they saw the ghost, and when they were brought to cried, "Save me take it away take it away."

One time a boy came to the house to spend Christmas. He was just a terror, was this boy. He had been a District

Telegraph Messenger boy, and he wasn't afraid of anything. The folks told him about the ghost, but he said he didn't care for any living ghost, and had just as soon see him as not.

That night the boy woke up, and saw the ghost standing in his bedroom, and he said, "Thishyer is nice corduct, coming into a gentleman's room without knocking. What do you want, anyway?"

The ghost replied in the most respectful way that he wanted to find the owner of the umbrella. "I stole that umbrella when I was alive," he said, "and I am filled with remorse."

"I should think you would be," said the boy, "for it is the worst old cotton umbrella I ever saw."

"If I can only find the owner and give it back to him," continued the ghost, "I can get a little rest; but I've been looking for him for ninety years, and I can't find him."

"Serves you right," said the boy, "for not sending for a messenger. You're in luck to meet me. Gimme the umbrella, and I'll give it back to the owner."

"Bless you," said the ghost, handing the umbrella to the boy; "you have saved me. Now I will go away and rest," and he turned to go out of the door, when the boy said,

"See here; it's fifty cents for taking an umbrella home, and I've got to be paid in advance."

" But I haven't got any money," said the ghost.

"Can't help that," said the boy. " You give me fifty cents, or else take your umbrella back again. We don't do any work in our office for nothing."

Well, the end of it all was that the ghost left the umbrella with the boy, and the next night he came back with the money, though where he got it nobody will ever know. The boy kept the money, and threw the umbrella away, for he was a real bad boy, and only made believe that he was going to find the owner, and the ghost was never seen again.

But I haven't told about the trouble with Aunt Eliza yet. The day she came to our house mother bought a lot of live crabs from a man, and put them in a pail in the kitchen. Tom McGinnis was spending the day with me, and I said to him what fun it would be to have crab races, such as we used to have down at the sea-shore last summer. He said wouldn't it, though; so each of us took three crabs, and went up-stairs into the spare bedroom, where we could be sure of not being disturbed. We had a splendid time with the crabs, and I won more than half the races. All of a sudden I heard mother calling me, and Tom and I just dropped the crabs into an empty work-basket, and pushed it under the sofa out of sight, and then went down-stairs.

I meant to get the crabs and take them back to the

HE PINCHED JUST AS HARD AS HE COULD PINCH.

kitchen again, but I forgot all about it, for Aunt Eliza came just after mother had called me, and everybody was busy talking to her. Of course she was put into the spare room, and as she was very tired, she said she'd lie down on the sofa until dinner-time and take her hair down.

About an hour afterwards we heard the most dreadful cries from Aunt Eliza's room, and everybody rushed upstairs, because they thought she must certainly be dead. Mother opened the door, and we all went in. Aunt Eliza was standing in the middle of the floor, and jumping up and down, and crying and shrieking at the top of her voice. One crab was hanging on to one of her fingers, and he pinched just as hard as he could pinch, and there were two more hanging on to the ends of her hair. You see, the crabs had got out of the work-basket, and some of them had climbed up the sofa while Aunt Eliza was asleep.

Of course they said it was all my fault, and perhaps it was. But I'd like to know if it's a fair thing to leave crabs where they can tempt a fellow, and then to be severe with him when he forgets to put them back. However, I forgive everybody, especially Aunt Eliza, who really doesn't mean any harm.

A PILLOW FIGHT.

WE'VE been staying at the sea-shore for a week, and having a beautiful time. I love the sea-shore, only it would be a great deal nicer if there wasn't any sea; then you wouldn't have to go in bathing. I don't like to go in bathing, for you get so awfully wet, and the water chokes you. Then there are ticks on the sea-shore in the grass. A tick is an insect that begins and bites you, and never stops till you're all ettup, and then you die, and the tick keeps on growing bigger all the time.

There was once a boy and a tick got on him and bit him, and kept on biting for three or four days, and it ettup the boy till the tick was almost as big as the boy had been, and the boy wasn't any bigger than a marble, and he died, and his folks felt dreadfully about it. I never saw a tick, but I know that there are lots of them on the sea-shore, and that's reason enough not to like it.

We stayed at a boarding-house while we were at the sea-shore. A boarding-house is a place where they give you pure country air and a few vegetables and a little meat, and I say give me a jail where they feed you if they do keep you shut up in the dark. There were a good many people in our boarding-house, and I slept up-stairs on the third story with three other boys, and there were two more boys on the second story, and that's the way all the trouble happened.

There is nothing that is better fun than a pillow fight; that is, when you're home and have got your own pillows, and know they're not loaded, as Mr. Travers says. He was real good about it, too, and I sha'n't forget it, for 'most any man would have been awfully mad, but he just made as if he didn't care, only Sue went on about it as if I was the worst boy that ever lived.

You see, we four boys on the third story thought it would be fun to have a pillow fight with the two boys on the second story. We waited till everybody had gone to bed, and then we took our pillows and went out into the hall just as quiet as could be, only Charley Thompson he fell over a trunk in the hall and made a tremendous noise. One of the boarders opened his door and said who's there, but we didn't answer, and presently he said "I suppose it's that cat people ought to be ashamed of themselves to keep such animals," and shut his door again.

After a little while Charley was able to walk, though his legs were dreadfully rough where he'd scraped them against the trunk. So we crept down-stairs and went into the boys' room, and began to pound them with the pillows.

They knew what was the matter, and jumped right up and got their pillows, and went at us so fierce that they drove us out into the hall. Of course this made a good deal of noise, for we knocked over the wash-stand in the room, and upset a lot of lamps that were on the table in the hall, and every time I hit one of the boys he would say "Ouch!" so loud that anybody that was awake could hear him. We fought all over the hall, and as we began to get excited we made so much noise that Mr. Travers got up and came out to make us keep quiet.

It was pretty dark in the hall, and though I knew Mr. Travers, I thought he couldn't tell me from the other boys, and I thought I would just give him one good whack on the head, and then we'd all run up-stairs. He wouldn't know who hit him, and, besides, who ever heard of a fellow being hurt with a pillow?

So I stood close up by the wall till he came near me, and then I gave him a splendid bang over the head. It sounded as if you had hit a fellow with a club, and Mr. Travers dropped to the floor with an awful crash, and never spoke a word.

I never was so frightened in my life, for I thought Mr. Travers was killed. I called murder help fire, and every

I NEVER WAS SO FRIGHTENED IN MY LIFE.

body ran out of their rooms, and fell over trunks, and there was the most awful time you ever dreamed of. At last somebody got a lamp, and somebody else got some water and picked Mr. Travers up and carried him into his room, and then he came to and said, " Where am I Susan what is the matter O now I know."

He was all right, only he had a big bump on one side of his head, and he said that it was all an accident, and that he wouldn't have Sue scold me, and that it served him right for not remembering that boarding-house pillows are apt to be loaded.

The next morning he made me bring him my pillow, and then he found out how it came to hurt him. All the chicken bones, and the gravel-stones, and the chunks of wood that were in the pillow had got down into one end of it while we were having the fight, and when I hit Mr. Travers they happened to strike him on his head where it was thin, and knocked him senseless. Nobody can tell how glad I am that he wasn't killed, and it's a warning to me never to have pillow fights except with pillows that I know are not loaded with chicken bones and things.

I forgot to say that after that night my mother and all the boys' mothers took all the pillows away from us, for they said they were too dangerous to be left where boys could get at them.

SUE'S WEDDING.

SUE ought to have been married a long while ago. That's what everybody says who knows her. She has been engaged to Mr. Travers for three years, and has had to refuse lots of offers to go to the circus with other young men. I have wanted her to get married, so that I could go and live with her and Mr. Travers. When I think that if it hadn't been for a mistake I made she would have been married yesterday, I find it dreadfully hard to be resigned. But we ought always to be resigned to everything when we can't help it.

Before I go any further I must tell about my printing-press. It belonged to Tom McGinnis, but he got tired of it and sold it to me real cheap. He was going to write to the YOUNG PEOPLE'S Post-office Box and offer to exchange it for a bicycle, a St. Bernard dog, and twelve good books, but he finally let me have it for a dollar and a half.

It prints beautifully, and I have printed cards for ever so many people, and made three dollars and seventy cents already. I thought it would be nice to be able to print circus bills in case Tom and I should ever have another circus, so I sent to the city and bought some type morn-aninch high, and some beautiful yellow paper.

Last week it was finally agreed that Sue and Mr. Travers should be married without waiting any longer. You should have seen what a state of mind she and mother were in. They did nothing but buy new clothes, and sew, and talk about the wedding all day long. Sue was determined to be married in church, and to have six bridesmaids and six bridegrooms, and flowers and music and things till you couldn't rest. The only thing that troubled her was mak-ing up her mind who to invite. Mother wanted her to invite Mr. and Mrs. McFadden and the seven McFadden girls, but Sue said they had insulted her, and she couldn't bear the idea of asking the McFadden tribe. Everybody agreed that old Mr. Wilkinson, who once came to a party at our house with one boot and one slipper, couldn't be invited; but it was decided that every one else that was on good terms with our family should have an invi-tation.

Sue counted up all the people she meant to invite, and there was nearly three hundred of them. You would hardly believe it, but she told me that I must carry around all the invitations and deliver them myself. Of course I couldn't do this without neglecting my studies and losing time, which is always precious, so I thought of a plan which would save Sue the trouble of directing three hundred invitations and save me from wasting time in delivering them.

I got to work with my printing-press, and printed a dozen splendid big bills about the wedding. When they were printed I cut a lot of small pictures of animals and ladies riding on horses out of some old circus bills and pasted them on the wedding bills. They were perfectly gorgeous, and you could see them four or five rods off. When they were all done I made some paste in a tin pail, and went out after dark and pasted them in good places all over the village. I put one on Mr. Wilkinson's front-door, and one on the fence opposite the McFaddens' house, so they would be sure to see it.

The next afternoon father came into the house looking very stern, and carrying one of the wedding bills in his hand. He handed it to Sue and said, "Susan, what does this mean? These bills are pasted all over the village, and there are crowds of people reading them." Sue read the bill, and then she gave an awful shriek, and fainted away, and I hurried down to the post-office to see if the mail had come in. This is what was on the wedding bills, and I am sure it was spelled all right:

SHE GAVE AN AWFUL SHRIEK AND FAINTED AWAY.

Miss Susan Brown announces that she will marry
Mr. James Travers
at the Church next Thursday at half past seven, sharp.
All the Friends of the Family
With the exception of
the McFadden tribe and old Mr. Wilkinson
are invited.
Come early and bring
Lots of Flowers.

Now what was there to find fault with in that? It was
printed beautifully, and every word was spelled right, with
the exception of the name of the church, and I didn't put
that in because I wasn't quite sure how to spell it. The bill
saved Sue all the trouble of sending out invitations, and it
said everything that anybody could want to know about
the wedding. Any other girl but Sue would have been
pleased, and would have thanked me for all my trouble,
but she was as angry as if I had done something real bad.
Mr. Travers was almost as angry as Sue, and it was the first
time he was ever angry with me. I am afraid now that he
won't let me ever come and live with him. He hasn't said
a word about my coming since the wedding bills were put
up. As for the wedding, it has been put off, and Sue says
she will go to New York to be married, for she would perfectly die if she were to have a wedding at home after that

boy's dreadful conduct. What is worse, I am to be sent away to boarding-school, and all because I made a mistake in printing the wedding bills without first asking Sue how she would like to have them printed.

OUR NEW DOG.

I'VE had another dog. That makes three dogs that I've had, and I haven't been allowed to keep any of them. Grown-up folks don't seem to care how much a boy wants society. Perhaps if they were better acquainted with dogs they'd understand boys better than they do.

About a month ago there were lots of burglars in our town, and father said he believed he'd have to get a dog. Mr. Withers told father he'd get a dog for him, and the next day he brought the most beautiful Siberian bloodhound you ever saw.

The first night we had him we chained him up in the yard, and the neighbors threw things at him all night. Nobody in our house got a wink of sleep, for the dog never stopped barking except just long enough to yell when something hit him. There was mornascuttleful of big lumps of coal in the yard in the morning, besides seven old boots, two chunks of wood, and a bushel of broken crockery.

Father said that the house was the proper place for the dog at night; so the next night we left him in the front hall. He didn't bark any all night, but he got tired of staying in the front hall, and wandered all over the house. I suppose he felt lonesome, for he came into my room, and got on to the bed, and nearly suffocated me. I woke up dreaming that I was in a melon patch, and had to eat three hundred green watermelons or be sent to jail, and it was a great comfort when I woke up and found it was only the dog. He knocked the water-pitcher over with his tail in the morning, and then thought he saw a cat under my bed, and made such an awful noise that father came up, and told me I ought to be ashamed to disturb the whole family so early in the morning. After that the dog was locked up in the kitchen at night, and father had to come down early and let him out, because the cook didn't dare to go into the kitchen.

We let him run loose in the yard in the daytime, until he had an accident with Mr. Martin. We'd all been out to take tea and spend the evening with the Wilkinsons, and when we got home about nine o'clock, there was Mr. Martin standing on the piazza, with the dog holding on to his cork-leg. Mr. Martin had come to the house to make a call at about seven o'clock, and as soon as he stepped on the piazza the dog caught him by the leg without saying a word. Every once in a while the dog would let go just long enough to spit out a few pieces of cork and take a fresh

HOW THAT DOG DID PULL!

hold, but Mr. Martin didn't dare to stir for fear he would take hold of the other leg, which of course would have hurt more than the cork one. Mr. Martin was a good deal tired and discouraged, and couldn't be made to understand that the dog thought he was a burglar, and tried to do his duty, as we should all try to do.

The way I came to lose the dog was this: Aunt Eliza came to see us last week, and brought her little boy Harry, who once went bee-hunting with me. Harry, as I told you, is six years old, and he isn't so bad as he might be considering his age. The second day after they came, Harry and I were in Tom McGinnis's yard, when Tom said he knew where there was a woodchuck down in the pasture, and suppose we go and hunt him. So I told Harry to go home and get the dog, and bring him down to the pasture where Tom said the woodchuck lived. I told him to untie the dog—for we had kept him tied up since his accident with Mr. Martin—and to keep tight hold of the rope, so that the dog couldn't get away from him. Harry said he'd tie the rope around his waist, and then the dog couldn't possibly pull it away from him, and Tom and I both said it was a good plan.

Well, we waited for that boy and the dog till six o'clock, and they never came. When I got home everybody wanted to know what had become of Harry. He was gone and the dog was gone, and nobody knew where they were, and Aunt Eliza was crying, and said she knew that horrid dog had eaten her boy up. Father and I and Mr. Travers had to go and hunt for Harry. We hunted all over the town, and at last a man told us that he had seen a boy and a dog going on a run across Deacon Smith's corn-field. So we went through the corn-field and found their track, for they had broken down the corn just as if a wagon had driven through it. When we came to the fence on the other side of the field we found Harry on one side of the fence and the dog on the other. Harry had tied the dog's rope round his waist, and couldn't untie it again, and the dog had run away with him. When they came to the fence the dog had squeezed through a hole that was too small for Harry, and wouldn't come back again. So they were both caught in a trap. How that dog did pull! Harry was almost cut in two, for the dog kept pulling at the rope all the time with all his might.

When we got home Aunt Eliza said that either she or that brute must leave, and father gave the dog away to the butcher. He was the most elegant dog I ever had, and I don't suppose I shall ever have another.

LIGHTNING.

Mr. Franklin was one of the greatest men that ever lived. He could carry a loaf of bread in each hand and eat another, all at the same time, and he could invent anything that anybody wanted, without hurting himself or cutting his fingers. His greatest invention was lightning, and he invented it with a kite. He made a kite with sticks made out of telegraph wire, and sent it up in a thunderstorm till it reached where the lightning is. The lightning ran down the string, and Franklin collected it in a bottle, and sold it for ever so much money. So he got very rich after a while, and could buy the most beautiful and expensive kites that any fellow ever had.

I read about Mr. Franklin in a book that father gave me. He said I was reading too many stories, and just you take this book and read it through carefully and I hope it will do you some good anyway it will keep you out of mischief.

I thought that it would please father if I should get some lightning just as Franklin did. I told Tom McGin nis about it, and he said he would help if I would give him half of all I made by selling the lightning. I wouldn't do this, of course, but finally Tom said he'd help me anyhow, and trust me to pay him a fair price; so we went to work.

We made a tremendously big kite, and the first time there came a thunder-storm we put it up; but the paper got wet, and it came down before it got up to the lightning. So we made another, and covered it with white cloth that used to be one of Mrs. McGinnis's sheets, only Tom said he knew she didn't want it any more.

We sent up this kite the next time there was a thunder-storm, and tied the string to the second-story window where the blinds hook on, and let the end of the string hang down into a bottle. It only thundered once or twice, but the lightning ran down the string pretty fast, and filled the bottle half full.

It looked like water, only it was a little green, and when it stopped running into the bottle we took the lightning down-stairs to try it. I gave a little of it to the cat to drink, but it didn't hurt her a bit, and she just purred. At last Tom said he didn't believe it would hurt anything; so he tasted some of it, but it didn't hurt him at all.

The trouble was that the lightning was too weak to do any harm. The thunder-shower had been such a little one

WE HURRIED INTO THE ROOM.

that it didn't have any strong lightning in it; so we threw away what was in the bottle, and agreed to try to get some good strong lightning whenever we could get a chance.

It didn't rain for a long time after that, and I nearly forgot all about Franklin and lightning, until one day I heard Mr. Travers read in the newspaper about a man who was found lying dead on the road with a bottle of Jersey lightning, and that, of course, explains what was the matter with him my dear Susan. I understood more about it than Susan did, for she does not know anything about Franklin being a girl, though I will admit it isn't her fault. You see, the cork must have come out of the man's bottle, and the lightning had leaked out and burned him to death.

The very next day we had a tremendous thunder-shower, and I told Tom that now was the time to get some lightning that would be stronger than anything they could make in New Jersey. So we got the kite up, and got ourselves soaked through with water. We tied it to the window-ledge just as we did the first time, and put the end of the string in a tin pail, so that we could collect more lightning than one bottle would hold. It was so cold standing by the window in our wet clothes that we thought we'd go to my room and change them.

All at once there was the most awful flash of lightning and the most tremendous clap of thunder that was ever heard. Father and mother and Sue were down-stairs, and they rushed up-stairs crying the darling boy is killed. That meant me. But I wasn't killed, neither was Tom, and we hurried into the room where we were collecting lightning to see what was the matter. There we found the tin pail knocked into splinters and the lightning spilled all over the floor. It had set fire to the carpet, and burned a hole right through the floor into the kitchen, and pretty much broke up the whole kitchen stove.

Father cut the kite-string and let the kite go, and told me that it was as much as my life was worth to send up a kite in a thunder-storm. You see, so much lightning will come down the string that it will kill anybody that stands near it. I know this is true, because father says so, but I'd like to know how Franklin managed. I forgot to say that father wasn't a bit pleased.

MY CAMERA.

I HAD a birthday last week. When I woke up in the morning I found right by the side of my bed a mahogany box, with a round hole on one side of it and a ground-glass door on the other side. I thought it was a new kind of rat-trap; and so I got out of bed and got a piece of cheese, and set the trap in the garret, which is about half full of rats. But it turned out that the box wasn't a rat-trap. Mr. Travers gave it to me, and when he came to dinner he explained that it was a camera for taking photographs, and that it would improve my mind tremendously if I would learn to use it.

I soon found out that there isn't anything much better than a camera, except, of course, a big dog, which I can't have, because mother says a dog tracks dirt all over the house, and father says a dog is dangerous, and Sue says a dog jumps all over you and tears your dresses a great good-for-nothing ugly beast. It's very hard to be kept apart from dogs; but our parents always know what is best for us, though we may not see it at the time; and I don't believe father really knows how it feels when your trousers are thin and you haven't any boots on, so it stings your legs every time.

But I was going to write about the camera. You take photographs with the camera—people and things. There's a lens on one end of it, and when you point it at anything, you see a picture of it upside down on the little glass door at the back of the camera. Then you put a dry plate, which is a piece of glass with chemicals on it, in the camera, and then you take it out and put it in some more chemicals, the right name of which is a developer, and then you see a picture on the dry plate, only it is right side up, and not like the one on the ground-glass door.

It's the best fun in the world taking pictures; and I can't see that it improves your mind a bit—at least not enough to worry you. You have to practise a great deal before you can take a picture, and everybody who knows anything about it tells you to do something different. There are five men in our town who take photographs, and each one tells me to use a different kind of dry plate and a different kind of developer, and that all the other men may mean well, and they hope they do, but people ought not to tell a boy to use bad plates and poor developers; and don't you pay any attention to them, Jimmy, but do as I tell you.

I've got so now that I make beautiful pictures. I took a photograph of Sue the other day, and another of old Deacon Brewster, and you can tell which is which just as easy as anything, if you look at them in the right way, and remember that Deacon Brewster, being a man, is smoking a pipe, and that, of course, a picture of Sue wouldn't have a pipe in it. Sue don't like to have me take pictures, but that's because she is a girl, and girls haven't the kind of minds that can understand art. Mr. McGinnis—Tom's father—don't like my camera either; but that's because he is near-sighted, and thought it was a gun when I pointed it at him, and he yelled, "Don't shoot, for mercy's sake!" and went out of our front yard and over the fence in less-enasecond. When he found out what it was he said he never dreamed of being frightened, but had business down-town, and he didn't think boys ought to be trusted with such things. anyway.

I made a great discovery last week. You know I said that when you look through the camera at anything you see it upside down on the ground glass. This doesn't look right, and unless you stand on your head when you take a photograph, which is very hard work, you can't help feel-ing that the picture is all wrong. I was going to take a photograph of a big engraving that belongs to father, when I thought of turning it upside down. This made it look all right on the ground glass. This is my discovery; and if men who take photographs could only get the people they photograph to stand on their heads, they would **get** beautiful pictures. Mr. Travers says that I ought **to** get a patent for this discovery, but so **far it** has only got me into trouble.

Saturday afternoon everybody was out of the house except me and the baby and the nurse, and she was down in the kitchen, and the baby was asleep. So I thought I would take a picture of the baby. Of course it wouldn't sit still for me; so I thought of the way the Indians strap their babies to a flat board, which keeps them from getting round-shouldered, and is very convenient besides. I got a nice flat piece of board and tied the baby to it, and put him on a table, and leaned him up against the wall. Then I remembered my discovery, and just stood the baby on his head so as to get a good picture of him.

I did get a beautiful picture. At least I am sure it would have been if I hadn't been interrupted while I was developing it. I forgot to put the baby right side up, and in about ten minutes mother came in and found it, and then she came up into my room and interrupted me. Father came home a little later and interrupted me some more. So the picture was spoiled, and so was father's new rattan. Of course I deserved it for forgetting the baby;

I DID GET A BEAUTIFUL PICTURE.

but it didn't hurt it any to stand on its head a little while, for babies haven't any brains like boys and grown-up people, and, besides, it's the solemn truth that I meant to turn the baby right side up, only I forgot it.

FRECKLES.

AFTER the time I tried to photograph the baby, my camera was taken away from me and locked up for ever so long. Sue said I wasn't to be trusted with it and it would go off some day when you think it isn't loaded and hurt somebody worse than you hurt the baby you good-for-nothing little nuisance.

Father kept the camera locked up for about a month, and said when I see some real reformation in you James you shall have it back again. But I shall never have it back again now, and if I did, it wouldn't be of any use, for I'm never to be allowed to have any more chemicals. Father is going to give the camera to the missionaries, so that they can photograph heathen and things, and all the chemicals I had have been thrown away, just because I made a mistake in using them. I don't say it didn't serve me right, but I can't help wishing that father would change his mind.

I have never said much about my other sister, Lizzie, because she is nothing but a girl. She is twelve years old, and of course she plays with dolls, and doesn't know enough to play base-ball or do anything really useful. She scarcely ever gets me into scrapes, though, and that's where Sue might follow her example. However, it was Lizzie who got me into the scrape about my chemicals, though she didn't mean to, poor girl.

One night Mr. Travers came to tea, and everybody was talking about freckles. Mr. Travers said that they were real fashionable, and that all the ladies were trying to get them. I am sure I don't see why. I've mornamiilion freckles, and I'd be glad to let anybody have them who would agree to take them away. Sue said she thought freckles were perfectly lovely, and it's a good thing she thinks so, for she has about as many as she can use; and Lizzie said she'd give anything if she only had a **few** nice freckles on her cheeks.

Mother asked what made freckles, and Mr. Travers said the sun made them just as it makes photographs. "Jimmy will understand it," said Mr. Travers. "He knows how the sun makes a picture when it shines on a photograph plate, and all his freckles were made just in the same way. Without the sun there wouldn't be any freckles."

This sounded reasonable, but then Mr. Travers forgot all about chemicals. As I said, the last time I wrote, chemicals is something in a bottle like medicine, and you have to put it on a photograph plate so as to make the picture that the sun has made show itself. Now if chemicals will do this with a photograph plate, it ought to do it with a girl's cheek. You take a girl and let the sun shine on her cheek, and put chemicals on her, and it ought to bring out splen did freckles.

I'm very fond of Lizzie, though she is a girl, because she minds her own business, and don't meddle with my things and get me into scrapes. I'd have given her all my freckles if I could, as soon as I knew she wanted them, and as soon as Mr. Travers said that freckles were made just like photo graphs, I made up my mind I would make some for her. So I told her she should have the best freckles in town if she'd come up to my room the next morning, and let me expose her to the sun and then put chemicals on her.

Lizzie has confidence in me, which is one of her best qualities, and shows that she is a good girl. She was so pleased when I promised to make freckles for her; and as soon as the sun got up high enough to shine into my win dow she came up to my room all ready to be freckled.

I exposed her to the sun for six seconds. I only exposed my photograph plates three seconds, but I thought that Lizzie might not be quite as sensitive, and so I exposed her longer. Then I took her into the dark closet where I kept the chemicals, and poured chemicals on her cheeks. I made her hold her handkerchief on her face so that the chemicals

MOTHER AND SUE MADE A DREADFUL FUSS.

couldn't get into her eyes and run down her neck, for she wanted freckles only on her cheeks.

I watched her very carefully, but the freckles didn't come out. I put more chemicals on her, and rubbed it in with a cloth; but it was no use, the freckles wouldn't come. I don't know what the reason was. Perhaps I hadn't exposed her long enough, or perhaps the chemicals was weak. Anyway, not a single freckle could I make.

So after a while I gave it up, and told her it was no use, and she could go and wash her face. She cried a little because she was disappointed, but she cried more afterwards. You see, the chemicals made her cheek almost black, and she couldn't wash it off. Mother and Sue made a dreadful fuss about it, and sent for the doctor, who said he thought it would wear off in a year or so, and wouldn't kill the child or do her very much harm.

This is the reason why they took my chemicals away, and promised to give my camera to the missionaries. All I meant was to please Lizzie, and I never knew the chemicals would turn her black. But it isn't the first time I have tried to be kind and have been made to suffer for it.

SANTA CLAUS.

The other day I was at Tom McGinnis's house, and he had some company. He was a big boy, and something like a cousin of Tom's. Would you believe it, that fellow said there wasn't any Santa Claus?

Now that boy distinctly did tell—but I won't mention it. We should never reveal the wickedness of other people, and ought always to be thankful that we are worse than anybody else. Otherwise we should be like the Pharisee, and he was very bad. I knew for certain that it was a fib Tom McGinnis's cousin told. But all the same, the more I thought about it the more I got worried.

If there is a Santa Claus—and of course there is—how could he get up on the top of the house, so he could come down the chimney, unless he carried a big ladder with him; and if he did this, how could he carry presents enough to fill mornahundred stockings? And then how could he help getting the things all over soot from the chimney, and how does he manage when the chimney is all full of smoke and fire, as it always is at Christmas! But then, as the preacher says, he may be supernatural—I had to look that word up in the dictionary.

The story Tom McGinnis's cousin told kept on worrying me, and finally I began to think how perfectly awful it would be if there was any truth in it. How the children would feel! There's going to be no end of children at our house this Christmas, and Aunt Eliza and her two small boys are here already. I heard mother and Aunt Eliza talking about Christmas the other day, and they agreed that all the children should sleep on cot bedsteads in the back parlor, so that they could open their stockings together, and mother said, "You know, Eliza, there's a big fireplace in that room, and the children can hang their stockings around the chimney."

Now I know I did wrong, but it was only because I did not want the children to be disappointed. We should always do to others and so on, and I know I should have been grateful if anybody had tried to get up a Santa Claus for me in case of the real one being out of repair. Neither do I blame mother, though if she hadn't spoken about the fireplace in the way she did, it would never have happened. But I do think that they ought to have made a little allowance for me, since I was only trying to help make the Christmas business successful.

It all happened yesterday. Tom McGinnis had come to see me, and all the folks had gone out to ride except Aunt Eliza's little boy Harry. We were talking about Christmas, and I was telling Tom how all the children were to sleep in the back parlor, and how there was a chimney there that was just the thing for Santa Claus. We went and looked at the chimney, and then I said to Tom what fun it would be to dress up and come down the chimney and pretend to be Santa Claus, and how it would amuse the children, and how pleased the grown-up folks would be, for they are always wanting us to amuse them.

Tom agreed with me that it would be splendid fun, and said we ought to practise coming down the chimney, so that we could do it easily on Christmas-eve. He said he thought I ought to do it, because it was our house; but I said no, he was a visitor, and it would be mean and selfish in me to deprive him of any pleasure. But Tom wouldn't do it. He said that he wasn't feeling very well, and that he didn't like to take liberties with our chimney, and, besides, he was afraid that he was so big that he wouldn't fit the chimney. Then we thought of Harry, and agreed that he was just the right size. Of course Harry said he'd do it when we asked him, for he isn't afraid of anything, and is so proud to be allowed to play with Tom and me that he would do anything we asked him to do.

Well, Harry took off his coat and shoes, and we all went up to the roof, and Tom and I boosted Harry till he got on the top of the chimney and put his legs in it and slid down. He went down like a flash, for he didn't know enough to brace himself the way the chimney-sweeps do. Tom and I we hurried down to the back parlor to meet him; but he had not arrived yet, though the fireplace was full of ashes and soot.

We supposed he had stopped on the way to rest; but after a while we thought we heard a noise, like somebody calling, that was a great way off. We went up on the roof, thinking Harry might have climbed back up the chimney, but he wasn't there. When we got on the top of the chimney we could hear him plain enough. He was crying and yelling for help, for he was stuck about half-way down the chimney, and couldn't get either up or down.

We talked it over for some time, and decided that the best thing to do was to get a rope and let it down to him, and pull him out. So I got the clothes-line and let it down, but Harry's arms were jammed close to his sides, so he couldn't get hold of it. Tom said we ought to make a slip-pernoose, catch it over Harry's head, and pull him out that way, but I knew that Harry wasn't very strong, and I was afraid if we did that he might come apart.

Then I proposed that we should get a long pole and push

Harry down the rest of the chimney, but after hunting all over the yard we couldn't find a pole that was long enough, so we had to give that plan up. All this time Harry was crying in the most discontented way, although we were doing all we could for him. That's the way with little boys. They never have any gratitude, and are always discontented.

As we couldn't poke Harry down, Tom said let's try to poke him up. So we told Harry to be patient and considerate, and we went down-stairs again, and took the longest pole we could find and pushed it up the chimney. Bushels of soot came down, and flew over everything, but we couldn't reach Harry with the pole. By this time we began to feel discouraged. We were awfully sorry for Harry, because, if we couldn't get him out before the folks came home, Tom and I would be in a dreadful scrape.

Then I thought that if we were to build a little fire the draught might draw Harry out. Tom thought it was an excellent plan. So I started a fire, but it didn't loosen Harry a bit, and when we went on the roof to meet him we heard him crying louder than ever, and saying that something was on fire in the chimney and was choking him. I knew what to do, though Tom didn't, and, to tell the truth, he was terribly frightened.

We ran down and got two pails of water, and poured

THEY GOT HARRY OUT ALL SAFE.

them down the chimney. That put the fire out, but you would hardly believe that Harry was more unreasonable than ever, and said we were trying to drown him. There is no comfort in wearing yourself out in trying to please little boys. You can't satisfy them, no matter how much trouble you take, and for my part I am tired of trying to please Harry, and shall let him amuse himself the rest of the time he is at our house.

We had tried every plan we could think of to get Harry out of the chimney, but none of them succeeded. Tom said that if we were to pour a whole lot of oil down the chimney it would make it so slippery that Harry would slide right down into the back parlor, but I wouldn't do it, because I knew the oil would spoil Harry's clothes, and that would make Aunt Eliza angry. All of a sudden I heard a carriage stop at our gate, and there were the grown folks, who had come home earlier than I had supposed they would. Tom said that he thought he would go home before his own folks began to get uneasy about him, so he went out of the back gate, and left me to explain things. They had to send for some men to come and cut a hole through the wall. But they got Harry out all safe; and after they found that he wasn't a bit hurt, instead of thanking me for all Tom and I had done for him, they seemed to think that I deserved the worst punishment I ever had, and I got it.

I shall never make another attempt to amuse children on Christmas-eve.

THE END

www.ingramcontent.com/pod-product-compliance
Lightning Source LLC
Chambersburg PA
CBHW020116030726

47498CB00006B/2133